Sia

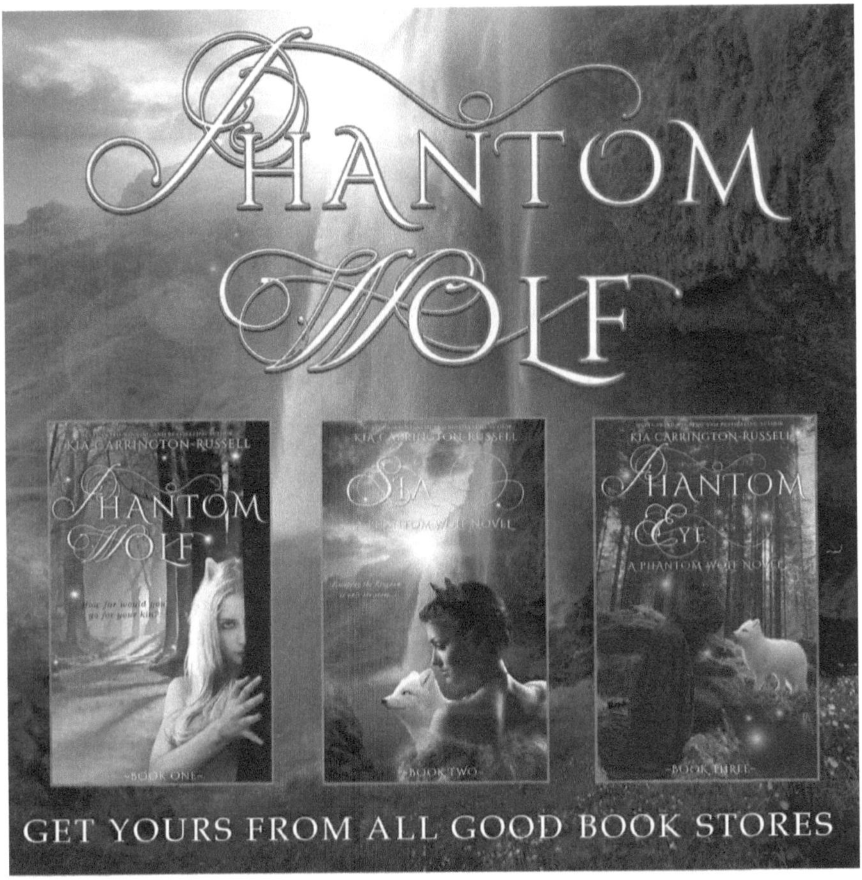
PHANTOM WOLF
KIA CARRINGTON-RUSSELL
PHANTOM WOLF
~BOOK ONE~
KIA CARRINGTON-RUSSELL
SIA
~BOOK TWO~
KIA CARRINGTON-RUSSELL
PHANTOM EYE
A PHANTOM WOLF NOVEL
~BOOK THREE~
GET YOURS FROM ALL GOOD BOOK STORES

Sia

Kia Carrington-Russell

Crystal Publishing

CRYSTAL PUBLISHING

Published by Crystal Publishing (Australia)

ISBN 978-0-6484981-1-7

Dedication

Thank you to all my supporters. This is now my fourth published book and I am really starting to embrace the enormity of being an author. I have had the pleasure of interacting regularly with my readers, who have supported me so spectacularly on my journey. Many of you have not physically met me, yet you have faith and kind words for me. Through your support I have gained confidence in my writing. I will continue to share my life and my writing with my readers so that I can continue to connect with people from all over the world. Words cannot denote my appreciation. You are all amazing.

For those who don't know: Sia, my main heroine, has been named after my loving, lifelong companion—a cavoodle. My sweet Sia.

Prologue from Phantom Wolf

As the sun had still not come up, I waited in the area that Trim usually met me in before training. I made sure that I didn't catch the scent of Kiba anywhere close; a few times he had approached me as I hid in the forest, but I ran from him. I still was unsure of how I felt or what to say. I wasn't sure I could trust in his confession.

Trim clumsily came to our meeting place, smiling and running toward me as he saw me waiting. I smiled back at the young boy. After many great meals and such long training, he had begun to grow small muscles, and he was now very talented with the stick he trained with.

"I have something for you," I said happily. Over the last few days I gathered the proper material like my papa once had for me. I pulled a knife out from behind my back that was wrapped with a large leaf. Trim's eyes widened as he took the gift hurriedly and opened it to reveal a stone blade. It had taken me a whole night to sharpen the blade and then another to strongly bind it with a handle.

In accordance with the tradition of my pack, I had inscribed my own name onto the handle. The bearer always wrote their name in the handle so the receiver had a memento of their mentor.

"Really?" he squealed. "Is it really for me?" He beamed as he began stomping his feet in some kind of excited dance, before running around me in circles. I laughed at the young boy, shaking my head.

"Of course it is for you," I said rubbing the orange hair on his head between his orange-furred ears. "Now let us go practice with it."

He radiated with excitement as he ran ahead of me to where we now trained. He fought gallantly against the tree with his new knife, cutting it eagerly.

I sat on a rock staring at him, watching as strike by strike he hit at the tree powerfully and precisely; sweat pouring off his face.

"You may have a break, Trim," I said firmly. If I didn't use such a forceful tone he would not stop. He gave me a dirty look, and then hid his face after I raised one of my eyebrows at him in challenge.

"Why do you want to be so strong, little one? You are only six years in age," I said as he came over to sit next to me. He lifted his body, his feet scuffling to reach atop the large rock I sat on.

"Because when I find a beautiful woman to entwine with, I will have a family to protect. And I want to be strong. I don't want anyone trying to steal our land. And Lady Momiko too... I will protect her. And you too, Sia; I am going to make you my wife," he beamed.

Taken aback, I gave him an awkward smile. *Such noble words for a young boy*. I rested my hand on his head, ruffling the hair between his orange ears.

"You will make a fine man one day and you will be very strong. I have no doubt in my mind," I said in all honesty. "But you mustn't try to impress me, Trim. I am already proud," I smiled.

Her Shadow

An innocent cub does not understand those looks that they
give me.

The impression they have of my frailness—misjudged. But
with caution they look at me.

It was not me whom they feared, but she whom I was named
after.

I am not directly linked to her, yet my life was saved because
of her.

Those who love me and are close cringe when they call my
name.

Amidst their darkest memories, I must find myself.

I must become my own being.

But in her shadow I shall always live.

Chapter One- Sia

This place is always serene enough to soothe my troubled mind, I thought to myself idly. I listened to the soothing sound of the powerful waterfall before me that was flowing into a clear pool of water below. The sky was clear and bright, with only a few clouds remaining from the terrific rain-storm we had endured only two nights before. Droplets of water lightly dripped around me, catching the sunlight as they fell elegantly from the luscious green foliage. The birds within the trees called out to others soaring high above me. The long grass below swayed in the gentle wind that tangled my long black hair. This was nature at its most tranquil. The air tasted fresh and I inhaled it deeply. I was at peace when I was here with only my own thoughts—free from the influence of others.

My attention was diverted to a movement in the water. I contentedly watched a shoal of fish glide through the water. A brown bear stalked them, anticipating their movement. My tail flickered back and forth as I watched from up high in a tree, admiring the bear's stealth as it skilfully caught one in its mouth. *To have so much freedom... To be able to provide for oneself...* My thoughts trailed off. That would be wonderful. I pined for the day when I would discover that for myself.

I glanced down at Ara's little white tail that was suddenly flickering back and forth. The hair on her back was rising, and she growled at someone who approached. Although only a small fox, her little canines were intimidating enough to deter anyone from stepping any closer. Her nose sniffed at the familiar scent. She recognized it just as I did and her growls instantly ceased.

"Sia!"

Trim's deep voice echoed around the trees as he impatiently searched through the shrubbery for me. I watched as the bear lifted its head at the sound of Trim's heavy footstep before pulling reluctantly away into the safety of the trees. I looked down at Trim, angry that he would disturb such a peaceful scene. Ara shifted on my lap, drawing his attention, and he looked up at me angrily through his one eye. He crossed his arms across his hard chest. His orange ears were pulled back and his large, vibrant tail was swishing with agitation. A branch from a nearby tree cast a shadow over the scar where his eye had once been.

"Your mother is yet again beside herself!"

"Oh, sweet ancestors of our land! Fear is stricken into the heart of Queen Keeley as her feral daughter, Sia, has once again run off. Oh, the loathing the people must have for such an odious action! And yet, I bet they don't even notice my disappearance," I said, dramatically falling back over the tree branch. I swung upside down, my legs attached to the tree so I would not fall. Trim instinctively held his hands out, expecting me to plummet to the ground below. I steadied myself and focused on his blue eye before crossing my arms. "But do not fear, my good people, for she always has her faithful bodyguard, Trim, to save her at the end of the day."

I flipped my legs over the tree branch so that I dropped suddenly. I closed my eyes against the sight of the ground rushing toward me. Trim caught me in his arms, as I knew he would. *What else would one expect from a Princess's bodyguard?* I thought sarcastically as he held me. I was suddenly aware of my naked body so close to his as he looked into my eyes.

His jawline tightened, exaggerating the stern appearance he seemed to favor. "Have you finished your theatrics yet?" he asked dryly while lowering me to the ground. "You are eighteen years of age in two days and yet you still act like a mere cub."

"You are only seven years my elder and yet you act as though your hair has turned gray," I retorted childishly. Although my accusation was immature and juvenile, it was not entirely groundless. He seemed immune to the flirtations of youth and was uninterested in other young wolves— despite how clearly they made known their intentions. I wondered at times if it was because he was more mature for his age. He was strong, independent, and competent. Women knew they could depend on him for protection, but his hard exterior barred anyone from getting close to him. His manly presence, coupled with his cool indifference, held an irresistible yet futile attraction for many women. Their adoring existence in the background was an irritation I had been accustomed to for far too long.

I pushed the unwelcome thoughts from my mind and affected an attitude of indifference that matched his. "I do not wish to go back home right now."

"Your father has requested I bring you back to the castle. They worry for you, Sia," he admonished me.

I walked toward the water's edge before crouching and wrapping my hands around my knees self-consciously. Ara sat beside me with one of her white paws resting on my leg. "King Saith—the kindest Alpha anyone has ever seen, credited with the almighty reunion between the packs of our divided land—desires *my* presence within the castle? How lucky I must be!" I chortled. My studied sarcasm masked my sadness. In truth, I was disappointed in myself for not living up to the status of my parents. They had both achieved greatness, and my self-deprecating demeanor disguised my feelings of inadequacy.

My mind fleeted over the past that was so familiar to me and yet so alien. Apparently there had been a time before my birth when my uncle Taleb reigned over the Kingdom. We were a divided land, and we were living in fear of the humans. The legend paralyzed our kind with fear—humans could curse a wolf, turning them instantly into a Phantom Wolf. Once cursed, the wolf would

12

hunt their pack and slaughter everyone within it. This fear was far too great for packs to deal with and it was that terror that divided our kind. Cracks began to appear—communities separated over disagreements of how best to protect their respective packs.

My father and Uncle Kiba were made outcasts by their parents for a sin they never committed. And because of that, Taleb killed my grandparents—whom I never even had the chance to meet. Taleb mistreated his subjects and after a long journey, my mother, Keeley, together with her best friend, Sia—the third Phantom Wolf—ended his kingship. Unfortunately, this was at the expense of the life of both Kiba and Sia. Their sacrifice was given freely to protect my unborn self, my parents, and a cub-sized Trim.

When Sia, the Phantom Wolf whom I was named after, killed Taleb, my father and mother came into power. Since then they have worked hard to unite all the packs under one kingdom again. Their monarchy valued peace instead of territorial ambushes and futile war. They emphasized equality and togetherness. Somehow this principle that was responsible for uniting so many only functioned to alienate me further. It was not an ambition I could share when they treated me like an outsider. I knew they did not answer all my questions truthfully. Their dedication was to my protection, not my knowledge or individuality.

My thoughts returned to Trim. He often reflected on those dark days. I could see he had lost his heart somewhere in the coldness. He shadowed himself in that darkness and devoted himself to protecting me. I learned as I grew older that his constant presence was borne out of a need to honor the sacrifice of those great wolves that had touched his young heart. Perhaps it was the enigma of his coldness that drew other wolves to him. He certainly seemed mysterious to me. To some, his disfigurement might seem repulsive, but those who knew him understood the scar as a mark of bravery. He had tried to defend Sia, but was clawed in the face, causing him to lose an eye. Without his scar he would be more handsome than most, but with it, well, it made him who he simply was. Trim. I would change nothing of his appearance; he was perfect. *But if only I could defrost his heart in the same way the sun melts the snow into the earth...* I wanted to know what he was thinking.

"Your parents have only ever given you love, I do not understand why you act so coldly toward them," Trim said harshly, interrupting my tender thoughts.

I was frustrated that no one listened to the reasons why I was upset. I was not really bitter toward my parents, only saddened as I felt they still held so much from me. Though why shouldn't Trim defend them? He was their greatest warrior and held in high regard. He had devoted himself to training and guarding me, yet it still burdened me that he could not comprehend my logic. I appreciated his loyalty to my parents, but I longed for his understanding. *Having spent so much time together, he should know why I feel like this. Or do we only spend empty time?*

I looked down at the ripples that spread across the water, hoping that he would not see the resentment in my light-blue eyes. I wondered briefly how he saw me. I had fair skin with a light scattering of freckles across my nose. I knew that to others my slight body—that so resembled my mother's in height and build— was a sign of fragility. No matter how much I willed myself to develop a womanly shape, I grew without curves. I flicked the water that reflected my appearance in disgust. I thought of all those that claimed I was the most exquisite wolf in the land. All I could see was the sharp contrast; the black fur of my ears and tail against my pale skin reminded me of night and day. My hair from my head trailed past my shoulders to my chest. My skin was so sickly white that I wondered if it alone was the reason why people thought me so fragile.

I didn't hate my parents; I loved them, but for far too long I had lived in the shadow of the legendary Phantom Wolf, Sia. Her name was now mine, and when people looked at me I often saw their eyes widen as they recalled her legend. Although she passed before I was even born, my existence prompted them to recall her story, her sacrifice. She had died to protect my family. I couldn't help but reflect on it as they spoke of her in hushed, reverent tones. My sense of inadequacy caused me to become defiant. I desperately fought to step out of her shadow into my own identity.

To Trim I was a mere task, a promise he had made. He had given his word at such a young age. As we grew together I made sure he was not aware how I pined for him. His only thoughts were of the promise he had made to her, and I knew it. I was only a reflection of her greatness. I remembered it each time I observed how pain clouded his eyes when my name was called.

I had now had these feelings for Trim for many years. At first I thought it to be only a childish infatuation. He was my friend, and I depended on his companionship. But the older I grew and the more time I spent with him, the more I knew it was not only friendship I craved. In so many ways he was stern, always lecturing me. But there were times when I had seen his sweeter side. I knew of his boundless compassion, loyalty, and selflessness. If I hadn't spent such time with him, I would have never known it to be there in the first place.

As I moved through the sensitive teenage years I became even more attached and began to fear that he would leave. I sought ways to reassure myself of his dedication. Around him I could excite myself, whether he realized it or not. When I ran away, he would always chase. It was nice to know that someone out there, no matter where I ran to or hid, would do anything within his power to find me. As my guard he was forced to do so, but as my heart changed and I became a woman, I realized the chase thrilled me for a far greater reason. And that was for him, a man, to follow me and search for me. And at times I was sure it was not only me that enjoyed it, but him as well.

I looked over my shoulder at him. He stood straight, a bow with feathered arrows strapped across his back and a sword resting on his hip. My eyes trailed down to the small knife strapped across his chest with Sia's name engraved on it. It was a gift she had bestowed upon him before she had died. Looking over his hard, bare chest and the knife that was so tightly strapped to him, I wondered if he would ever let me close to his heart.

"We will go," I said, no longer wanting to dwell in the depths of my sadness. I brushed my black braided hair over one side of my chest, wishing that it was long enough to completely conceal my annoyed expression. *Once again I must remain within the castles walls where I can be monitored, protected, and most importantly, lied to.*

Conversation at home was riddled with politics—that is, what conversation I was permitted to hear. Although all had been well for many years, over the past two years much of my parents' work had begun to erode. My father's alliance with other packs was deteriorating for no known reason. My father feared that perhaps the packs were reverting back to being territorial. It seemed our kind was regressing to when they had to segregate in an attempt to define their own packs— standing against each other in a show of strength. My father delegated more eyes on me, making sure my curious mind didn't lead me too far from the castle.

Trim and I walked through the small forest back to our castle in silence. The great cemented wall that encased our pack, our huts, and the castle itself was mighty. The huts for members of our pack who were not of our royal bloodline were made out of sticks and clay. The castle was made of some form of stone. It had stood for many hundreds of years and was beautifully maintained by those serving under my mother and father. I stood between the gates of the great wall that surrounded us. The path ahead led to the entrance of the castle. I looked to the right, contemplating an escape route. A path led to our castle's glorious gardens; it had been some time since I was able to go there. I noticed there was a few more newly-built huts nestled among the high plants that lined the path.

Trim stopped abruptly behind me as Ara waited by my side. My little Ara; I could not communicate with her in my own language, yet somehow she often knew what it was I spoke of or thought. I saved her at a young age when little cubs tried to hunt her for a feast. I could not condone it; from a young age I was infuriated by wolves who hunted more than what was needed. The beasts on our land should be respected and thanked for the food they provided us, not needlessly hunted. Luckily for us, the boars, deer, and birds repopulate at a wondrous rate, offering us a variety of meat. I was satisfied we would not be responsible for wiping out a species. In my eyes, we were all equal. Neither animal nor my kind should live in fear of one another. We should be able to run as one. I tried to walk away from Ara when I set her free, but she had followed me ever since; our bond was solidified and we enjoyed the closest of friendships.

I watched over some small cubs that were noisily chasing one another and running between Trim and me. It felt like a lifetime ago that Trim and I were so small. Although, it was not play he offered me; he simply chased me when I ran away, threatening to leave the castle grounds. I smiled after the children, thinking of how much fun I had torturing Trim in such a way.

Large oak doors opened wide for us as we entered the castle and Siesta, the wolf who attended to me, came running down the hall. She was only a few years older than me, with long light-brown fur and magnificent gray eyes. I could see the relief in her eyes as she drew nearer. I shivered as I waited in the hallway for her to reach us. The stone walls structured our castle well. There were many large windows to allow the sun in, but still some parts of the castle seemed gloomy and cold. It was a large, old building, and we had lined the hallways with torches. The flames only added to the eeriness.

Magnificent pictures of our ancestors framed the walls of the castle. Most of our furniture was chopped and carved by skilled wolves. They had created ornate tables, chairs, and bedframes. Although the castle was impressive and fit for royalty, I preferred the outdoors. There were many areas outside our castle which were beautiful, especially the garden. We had nice green grass for our training areas, and smaller areas where wolves could go for intimate celebrations. Most favored our spectacular garden which grew many different flowers from different regions. Much of the flora was given to us by packs with which we had formed allegiances.

"Oh my lady, you were gone for far too long this time!" Siesta fussed breathlessly, looking over to Trim in gratitude. Her eyes lingered for far too long, like they always did. "Thank you for retrieving her, Trim."

"As always, it is both my obligation and my pleasure to do so," he said, raising his arm and slightly bowing to her.

"That is not necessary inside my home," I sulked, irritated that he always acted so formally with others but taunted and lectured me.

"A lack of manners may be your shortcoming, young Princess, but it is not mine," Trim retorted sharply. I looked away from him, flushed; it was only ever me on the receiving end of his sharp tongue. He criticized me on my manners, curiosity, and unworldliness; once he had even called me "irrational."

"Lady Momiko was in search of you, Trim," Siesta said kindly, moving aside.

"Then I shall aid Lady Momiko," he said, striding toward the grand staircase.

"Trim, will I see you tomorrow for training?" I called out in a hopeful tone.

"You are to train with Hansel tomorrow," he said, brushing me off quickly. I did not show the anger on my face like I usually would. I had not shared my secret with anyone about how my heart truly ached for Trim and I was scared for even Siesta to see. It would feel like an even bigger failure if others knew my lack of success in persuading him to see me as a woman.

"My lady, your mother has requested for you to see her once you were back within the castle," Siesta said in a sweet voice. She had a soft spot for my mother and her voice was always full of love and respect when she spoke of her.

"How does Lady Momiko fare?" I asked as I began walking toward the library. If my mother was not with our pack attending to her daily duties, you could invariably find her hidden amongst books.

"She is still weak, my lady, I fear she is approaching her last few days," Siesta replied sadly.

I pushed down the lump within my throat, sad to hear that she may soon go. She was the last of Trim's pack after they dispersed many years ago. She was one of the few who approved of my adventurous nature. Her sharpness disguised the caring nature she held toward me. She was the one I ran to in order to heal my small wounds and injuries—self-inflicted, of course.

How would Trim bear this news? Would he once again pretend that everything was all right? Lady Momiko was the only person I had ever seen him cry in front of, and that was only once. I recalled the memory of the small teenage figure dropping to his knees, crying in front of her with confusion. I had watched from afar, only a mere child and desperately trying to understand that raw feeling of loss he held for the Phantom Wolf. I knew he struggled to understand this path she had set for him. Ever since then he had watched over me daily, amassing much respect and prestige amongst our pack for his skills in combat during training.

I opened the great doors to the library, which smelled strongly of the countless old books that detailed our ancestry. My eye caught the long jewel on my mother's tail that trailed behind her as she walked absentmindedly toward some chairs. Some books were opened near her seat by the fire. Her long brown hair covered her tail as she sat on the wooden chair.

To my left were long tables which had many books piled on them, four of them stretching toward the end of the room. On my right were tall wooden bookshelves. Our ancestors had been recording our history for a very long time. Most of our kind did not know how to read or write, but my mother had been taught by Trim. She herself had become literate within this very room. I looked over to the large painting on my left, which was created with odd colors. It ran from the ground to the ceiling and was stuck onto a thin wood. It stood as a memorial to The Great Phantom Wolf, Sia, and her lover, Kiba, who was also turned into a Phantom Wolf. I looked at his black fur. It was the same as mine, but his blue eyes were darker than my own. I was sure he would have been a wonderful uncle. Often I gave thanks to his portrait in remembrance of the sacrifice he made to protect my family.

"Mother," I called as I walked toward her, ready for yet another lecture for venturing away from the castle. I looked down at Ara for comfort. Her little blue eyes looked back up at me and her head tilted to the side in confusion.

My mother held her hands to her chest in concern as she spoke, "Sia, where have you been? It is only two days until the celebration of your age; you know we are soon to have guests. We will be surrounded by foreign packs. You cannot so carelessly parade yourself outside of our protection."

"My Queen, please excuse me," Siesta begged, raising her hand to her chest and pardoning herself as she left the room.

"I know, Mother, but it was only a short stroll. If anything were to eventuate from it I could very well look after myself. I am not a cub anymore. I can fight; you just choose not to see it," I challenged, resentful that no one noticed my skills.

"My dear, sweet Sia, you are my only cub. And a daughter I am proud of. I would appreciate if you kept that in mind when you decide to leave us for a 'stroll.' I know you can look after yourself but you know your father is uneasy because of the restlessness in our land. Please be more considerate." She stroked my long black hair. "You are a strong, radiant wolf. I believe in you with all my heart. But you must not risk your safety on curiosity."

"I understand, Mother," I said, my energy depleted. My shoulders sagged. Her emotive words always worked to her advantage. "I am sorry."

"No, my dear, I am sorry," she said her hand dropping from my thick black hair. She sat beside the fire, motioning for me to sit with her. My eyebrows knitted in confusion as to why she was apologizing.

"There is a pack approaching that is only a few days' hike from here. They are closest to the water near the land that I once came from. The pack has requested to come to your celebration. However, their Alpha wishes to try and unite our packs, through your hand and his son's," she explained hesitantly.

I stared at her for a while, shocked, my words stifled by my disbelief. "I beg your pardon?" I finally asked. I could not believe she would expect me to participate in such a sham. Perhaps I had heard her wrong. We were only to mate with one wolf in our lifetime and to expect me to do so for a political reason was disgusting. Once we physically entwined with another, we were forever connected with them—a link that could not be broken even in death. There was no chance of a second love with another. The entwinement of your mate would forever be your one and only. This bond was so deep that it anchored in the spirit world. Even after death you would forever be together. My own mother out of everyone should understand how seriously this commitment should be taken.

"It is as I said it is, but your father has no intention of consenting to such a thing. Your mate should be of your own choosing. But this is a great opportunity for your father to reach out to them and see whether they will align peacefully with this kingdom. An arranged entwinement is not our intention nor would we allow it. We just ask for you to be on your best behavior," she said, reaching her hand out to me. Her blue eyes were pleading as I pulled away from her and stood up from my seat.

"I am most disappointed you would even ask this of me." I did not appreciate being used as bait to form a political allegiance. I hated lies. Would she expect me to flirt? Lead them on? A lie would make me feel as though I could not be myself in the presence of this pack. When did we have to resort to tricking packs to come to our kingdom? My father had always stated it was of their own free will. Was this not deceit? Mostly I was sad to know they would ask this of me without revealing the true meaning behind it. "For what reason would you use me as your bait? Why are you trying to gather all these packs?"

My mother sagged in her chair once again, holding her hands on her lap. They were always so hesitant to tell me why they worked so hard toward the goal of assimilating all the separate packs into one large one. I always knew from a young age they were holding information from me, even when it came to the castle—there were sections in which I was forbidden to enter. Or they would whisper in secrecy to one another, ushering me away.

On nights when I could not sleep my father was far away on the borders of the land, mingling with other packs in the hope that they would come to live in our castle. I understood their goal but never the true meaning behind it. To me it felt as if they were trying to prepare for something. They dismissed any suspicions I dared to voice. Even Trim was within the inner circle of my father's trust. They never spoke of the truth, yet I was supposed to believe in their lies and stay behind the castle walls. All because of a belief that united my peers— an understanding from which I was exempt.

"I will not be part of your plan; especially one that is designed for a reason that is kept from me. If you cannot be honest with me, then my answer is 'no,'" I said, walking toward the door where my father stood.

He looked over to my mother with an expression of sadness. "Please do not speak to your mother like that," he spoke out in a tired voice while walking over to her and placing his hand on her shoulder. She patted it gently. Over the past two years his long black hair had begun to blur into gray from the stress of running our kingdom. His blue eyes flickered over the painting beside me. "I know you must be offended by us asking this of you. But we have no expectation of anything eventuating from it. Trim will still be close, just in case. We do not expect you to entwine with either one of them. The two brothers, I have heard, are both respectful, so when you reject them I think they will understand. But their interest in you will permit us enough time to talk to their Alpha, Kratin, and try to create an alliance."

"Now there are two? Not just one?" I spat, angry that they had already planned so much without my knowledge, much less my consent. Once again I was expected to live the life that was planned out for me, regardless of what it was I wanted.

"Yes Sia, there are two sons. But as we have already said, nothing will come of this. We would not allow such an insincere union to take place; you know we would never do that to you," my father said.

"Yet we will lie; we will pretend. What a father you are prepared to be in order to rule. Even suggestion is a lie and not one I will be a part of. I will not," I added angrily before storming out of the room. Ara barked at the two of them from behind me and then followed.

Trim stood against the wall of the hallway, one of his legs lifted and pressed into the wall, his hands crossed over his chest. He looked at me evenly with his one good eye as I walked past him haughtily. Wordlessly he slipped into the library to speak with my parents.

I walked down the hallway, then through the Great Hall— where we often celebrated and held feasts for our people—before finally reaching the solace of my personal wing of the castle. I almost ran through the dimly-lit entrance to my room before slamming the door behind Ara, still infuriated that they would ask such a thing of me. As my riled thoughts rolled through my mind, I pressed my back firmly against the door. I looked into Ara's small blue eyes, calming myself. She jumped onto my bed and coiled up at the end. I followed her lead and then brushed my hand through her silky fur. I felt my fangs tipping into my bottom lip. *I must have been pulling such an ugly face,* I realized.

As I calmed down I began to feel guilty that I had reacted in such a way toward my mother and father, for they wouldn't have asked this of me unless desperate. I sagged, feeling defeated. *If I only have to be well-mannered for a few days then surely I can do that.* Coiling around Ara, I stared at my ring-finger until I fell into an uneasy sleep.

Chapter Two- Further than the Walls

$\mathcal{I}$awoke to the sounds of whispers near my door. I was surprised to note I had slept for only a few hours. It was now dark outside. Ara must have heard the noises as well for she roused beside me, yawning and stretching out her front paws.

"I can hold onto this for her. I doubt she will be eating at the Great Hall tonight," Trim's voice rang out, startling me. He was outside my door.

"Of course," Siesta's voice responded. "Would you like me to keep you company as you wait for her to wake?"

"That is not necessary. Please thank the hunters and those who stewed this meal for Princess Sia in my stead, however," Trim kindly asked. Siesta agreed, her voice always softer when she spoke to Trim. I suspected she too had a fondness for him, although she had not yet confided in me.

There was an awkward shuffling and Siesta's light footsteps faded as she walked away from my room. I held my breath and did not move as I listened to Trim edging closer to my door.

"I know you're awake."

I frowned as I wondered how he could know such a thing. Before I knew it he had rudely opened my door, allowing himself in without my permission. "I did not permit you to enter," I huffed. I remained on my bed as he crossed the room, seemingly unperturbed by my tone. Ara was coiled in my arms. I continued stroking through her silky hair.

"You must eat, Sia," he said sternly, offering the bowl out to me from beside my bed. "Or your muscles will never grow."

I narrowed my eyes on him, agitated that he would mention my physical appearance. I had tried for many years to become stronger and larger, but I remained petite despite my efforts. "I do not wish to eat—nor have *you* in my presence right now. Your tone insults me," I said angrily, looking away from him.

His hand caught mine, taking me by surprise. I looked back into his blue eye. My heart pounded in my chest at his sudden touch. He slowly slipped the bowl of food into my hand. "Please eat. We have a challenging few days ahead of us. I cannot very well let a princess starve under my watch," he said, letting go of my hand. I looked into the stew, confused. "If you need anything, call on me. I will be outside your room over the next few days." Immediately I started to protest, but he quickly held up his hands and interrupted with, "This has already been arranged by your father."

"My room...? For what reason would you need to be so close? You have your own room within the castle walls," I exclaimed, my heart pounding at the thought of him being so close to me as I slept.

He evaded my question as he briskly crossed the room. "You will now train with me tomorrow morning, so please get a proper night's sleep. I will not take it easy on you tomorrow." When he reached the door, he hesitated with his hand on the handle and surprised me by looking back. "Good night, Sia," he said in a softer tone. He closed the door behind him, leaving me alone. The moonlight shone in from my open window and I looked down at Ara.

I reflected at length on the sudden change. Why did he have to be closer to me? I swallowed my excitement at his proximity. Although I trusted his judgment, I knew there was something he wasn't telling me. *He is as cold as always*, I reminded myself bitterly, *only now he is physically closer*.

Ara nudged her head against my stomach and I began stroking her fur once again. I gave thanks to the beast that had been sacrificed for the meal, thus giving me the nutrition I needed to survive. Ara's eyes had fixed on the food I had in my hand, like always. As usual I shared my meal with her. She did not care what food it was; if I were to eat it, then so was she.

I settled back to get some sleep. I felt an eeriness radiate through the castle that I tried to ignore. I dismissed it as my imagination. My confused mind swirled with thoughts and I could only manage a glimmer of sleep throughout the night.

*

"Good morning, my lady Sia," Siesta called out cheerfully as she barged into my room. She began lining jewels across the table against the wall. I squinted at the ray of sunlight that beamed through my window. My heart lifted as I listened to the beautiful bluebirds outside that whistled and welcomed morning. I stretched eagerly, yawning and letting my canines stretch past my lips as I stared out the window.

"Good Morning Siesta, and how do you fare this morning?" I focused on the jewels that she lined. "Why have you placed so many jewels along my table?"

"I fare well, my lady. These jewels were requested by your mother; it seems that Kratin and his pack are to arrive today. Your mother specifically told me to remind you that you must act the lady today. You are to dress accordingly."

"They come *today*?" I repeated, recalling the conversation with my parents from the previous night.

"Yes, my lady. I am very excited for you. You have grown very beautiful and your radiance is yet again proved by such a high and strong pack showing interest in you." She raised a long green gem to the sunlight in contemplation.

"I do not like any of the jewels," I stated bitterly. I did not want to go through with the charade. The thought left distaste in my mouth. The lie was lingering in the air already.

"Don't worry. Your attractiveness will diminish with each word you speak," Trim quipped, his wide shoulders barely fitting through my doorframe. His presence made my room seem smaller, as though there was less air to inhale.

"My words will be of no consequence. Only those who express a view that opposes my own shall encounter a different tone," I raised an eyebrow, implying he was the only adversary I anticipated.

"Of course, once again you are very right, Princess," he said dryly, his tone edging into sarcasm that apparently only I noticed. "Get up, you can select your finery and enhance your beauty later. For now, we train."

Before I could release the annoyed words that built on my tongue, Ara jumped out of my lap and followed him out. I jumped out of bed and followed, losing them quickly in the echoing hallways as I tried to match their rapid pace.

I walked out the front doors, greeting a few of the villagers who went about their morning chores. They looked at me with wide, dazzled eyes—more so than usual—for some unknown reason. I walked around the castle and into the small grassy area in which we often trained. If I looked from the window in my room I could see the tips of the green plants that enclosed this ground. Artists could fashion this kind of plant into any shape they wanted. A lot of these were in our great garden and the wolves maintained them with pride.

I walked into the green area and narrowed my eyes on the lonely Ara, who waited for us in the middle of the training area. As I stepped onto the grass she tilted her head at me in confusion. Playfully, I did the same, but my feet were instantly swept from underneath me. I landed on my back, coughing in shock.

"You must always be cautious and aware," Trim advised. He blocked the sun from my eyes as he came to my side and offered his hand out to me. I knocked it away, trying to gain my lost breath as I slowly stood up. I found I wasn't agitated, only fired up. I smiled in excitement. *So today he will take me seriously.*

I raised both my fists, rocking back and forth on my feet, anticipating his attacks. But he did nothing; he simply stood there with his hands behind his back, watching me. Annoyed, I threw my hands in the air. "So you won't take me seriously enough to want—"

Before I could finish, he grabbed my wrist and spun me around so that my arm was uncomfortably pinned behind my back. He had prevented me from looking into his face as I tried to speak. I could feel his body against mine. He had stopped me so violently from speaking anything further that I was now shocked into silence. I felt his light breaths on my shoulder as he whispered in my ear, "Never let impatience cloud your judgment about your pursuer's next move." Before I could question the meaning of his words, Trim loosened his grip on me and took a few steps back.

Ara now sat near the high plants, observing us with interest as we trained. I gained my stance again, rocking back and forth on my feet, ready for the fight. But once again he did nothing. I kicked high and just as I had anticipated he blocked my foot with his hand. His torso was left unprotected, just as I had planned, and I punched into his stomach. He stepped back, blocking my fist and diverting me to his left. He hit the back of my neck lightly, indicating my defeat. I looked back at him, agitated that I couldn't land my hit.

"You are only small; don't try to use your might against me. Use your *size* against me. Tire me out," Trim suggested as he clasped his hands behind his back once again. I balanced myself again before rocking back and forth on my feet, trying to understand what he had meant. We often trained in other ways. With a bow and arrow, I was fantastic, but my up-close fighting wasn't to the same standard as his. Although I could manage against most of the other guards with bare hand fighting, it was my goal to beat Trim, my mentor, from the very start. I could only handle small weapons such as knives; swords were too awkward for me to hold. Although I was trained well, larger weapons were not to my liking. I was simply too petite.

I slowly edged closer and closer to him before rounding my kick toward his stomach, but once again he had already anticipated my movement and blocked it. I kicked toward him, placing my foot down when I missed and therefore shortening the space between us. I leaned forward and then punched; he had already both his hands out to block my own. Strength wasn't my greatest asset but I was always fast. I assumed that was what he was implying—to use my smaller size against him, along with my speed, to exhaust him and gain an advantage.

I crouched low, kicking at his shins in one swift movement. He jumped beside me, bringing down his open hand above my head. I blocked it with both my hands, grabbing his wrist and pulling him toward me as I tried to knee him in the stomach. One of his knees rose, blocking my blow once again. I raised both my legs, holding onto his forearms and hoping my weight would be too heavy for him to still stand straight. If I could break his guarded stance then I might have a chance. Instead of his own arms sagging because of my weight, he clenched firmly, his arms bulking in strength as he held me up.

I took advantage of that, grabbing his shoulders and swinging myself over his back. I attempted to knee him in the back. Already he had blocked it, turning his attention on me once again. I raised my arms defensively as he punched back. I caught his hand, kicking into his shin. Once again I missed. He wrapped his hand around my wrist, pulling me toward his hard body and clasping me in his arms. I raised both my legs to his chest, kicking at him to break his grip. He released me and steadily took a step back, regaining his posture. I leapt for him, taking the opportunity to charge him. Just as I reached him he dropped into a crouch. He grabbed me roughly by my waist and pulled me with him as he rolled backward onto his back.

I clenched my hands tightly, ready to roll myself over, but he pulled me down and stretched me over the length of his body. His blue eye looked intently into mine as I breathed heavily in exhaustion. Suddenly he pushed me up into the air, balancing my body above his with his sheer strength. One of his hands held me up at my waist and the other was on my thigh. I looked down at him in confusion. Slowly he lowered me so that my outstretched arms touched the ground at either side of his neck. My hips touched his and my legs found the ground. I awkwardly lay over him, captivated by his beautiful blue eye and hard face.

The scar that etched so deeply into his skin may have been hideous to some, but it was an imperfection I loved. It showed his strength and courage. His hard eye reflected so much sorrow and confusion. But, for the first time, I thought Trim was actually looking at me—as a *woman*. His hot breaths captivated me as they steadied, and I was lost in anticipation.

"I want you to be more careful and remember to use your size against your opponent. Tire them... When you need strength, I will always be here, and you can always borrow mine. You will not have to rely on your own, but rely on mine instead. But still, do not put yourself in any uncertain situations," he said carefully, his hand reaching for my hair. I flinched under his touch, unsure as to why he was all of a sudden showing me affection.

"My lady?" a familiar voice called out, breaking the spell he had over me.

I awkwardly jumped upright and focused my attention on Hansel, who stood by the tall garden walls. His green eyes looked at us interrogatingly. Trim had just as quickly straightened himself in front of Hansel, whose tail stiffened in confusion as he looked between the two of us.

"Yes, Hansel?" I quickly asked, unsure as to why I was acting so strange—nothing had even happened.

"If you would allow me to continue with your training, your father has requested to see Trim for a few minutes," Hansel said, tightening his jaw as he looked at Trim.

Trim nodded ever so slightly and walked in the direction of the castle without looking back at me. When he was level with Hansel, almost shoulder-to-shoulder, he stopped and spoke in a low tone. "Her hand-to-hand has improved; I would recommend continuing her training with weaponry."

Hansel stepped forward without even looking at Trim, smiling brightly. "As Trim has suggested, my lady, shall we train with weapons?"

I shuddered involuntarily. His green eyes always lingered for far too long on me, making me feel uncomfortable. Although I understood him to be harmless—his manners were impeccable—there was something arrogant about him. He was certainly handsome in an obvious way with his honeycomb-colored hair, but he was too used to women's eyes on him. He had not yet found a mate and I suspected he endeavored to capture my attentions, even if I was a princess.

"Of course," I smiled lightly, while looking over his shoulder to Trim's retreating back.

"I have heard that we are expecting Kratin and his pack today. Apparently his sons have a certain interest in our very own princess. I hope the high expectation placed on your beauty does not trouble you," he said with a cunning smile.

"My beauty is not for other packs to judge," I said, annoyed. I was sick of hearing people place value on my appearance rather than my personality or my skills. The more I aged, the more it seemed others only wanted me to smile and sit prettily. I did not see what they gloated of. When I looked at myself I tried to see who they wanted me to be. *But that is not me, and slowly I must challenge others to see that as well,* I thought with determination. It was only Trim who did not judge me on my beauty but on my stealth, strength, and abilities as a wolf. *That is what I want to be judged by.*

"Ah, but you are beautiful, Princess, and your brawn and strength are just as wondrous. You will make a phenomenal queen one of these days," he said with a bright smile, his green eyes lingering on my thick black hair.

"You already have a queen," I snapped. My mother was an amazing queen and his tactic of flattery always grated on my nerves. I no longer wanted to be babied or manipulated in such a way. I wanted to run free and train by myself. The idea was too appealing to resist and I realized that while Trim was not close by I could escape the castle walls. The villagers lived inside huts that were enclosed by the castle's great walls, therefore providing me with an escape plan. There were warriors that guarded the wall but I had an escape route amongst the huts.

Irritated by his presence, I forced myself to smile at him. "Hansel, thank you for prioritizing my training above your duties. May I go for a quick break to enjoy some water? When I come back, shall we train intensely with weaponry? My left elbow drops under the weight of a sword."

"Princess Sia, if I may be so bold, last time you uttered these words you ran away and it took us half a day to find you."

"You would be correct in the assumption that you should not speak to me like that," I snapped. "But do not be so silly," I continued, softening my tone. "Why would I run away on such an important occasion? Kratin and his pack are soon to come. I will only be a few minutes, Hansel." I pardoned myself and Ara followed. Hansel tried to follow but Ara growled at him, warning him to stay back. He did not venture further than the entrance to the training grounds. I walked around the castle and toward the outskirts of the villagers' huts, still greeting them kindly. The huts were enclosed by the castle walls, and the people lived within the protection of these walls on royal ground.

As I casually walked between a few of the huts, I looked behind me to make sure no one followed. I walked over to the hut that was supported by the wall. It was Lady Momiko's hut, but she had been moved into the castle for treatment after becoming ill. Her home was now empty; the air dusty and stale. I looked around, saddened that she was no longer here. Often she would say to me when I walked in, "Are you sure this is a day you wish to run away?" Her crisp tone had always put a smile on my face. I dropped to my hands and knees and pulled back the small fur throw behind one of her bookshelves. It was her who created this escape hole for me, daring me to venture more. She always encouraged me to search for what it was I was missing. And yet my curiosity was never fully quenched.

I crawled through the small hole that tunneled into the cement wall. Lady Momiko had chiseled away the cement over time, creating an escape route for me. I pushed the bush aside that hid the hole on the other side, cautious that no one was on patrol. When I was certain we were alone, I prompted Ara to run toward the trees on the next hill. I ran after her, not looking back to see if anyone followed.

For now I must run, I must clear my thoughts.

I could run free and be myself... before I was expected to behave as though I were someone else for our guests.

Chapter Three- Difference in Packs

$\mathscr{I}$watched over the mother boar and her two babies who were foraging around the ground for food. I hid beneath some shrubbery. It was a bright day with a cool breeze and watching them contented me. I was fascinated by how they functioned differently from us and how they survived as a species. They didn't need weapons to hunt for food; they simply used their mouths and their sense of smell. The fact that their canines were on the outside of their body, near their snouts, was amazing.

Trim's familiar scent reached my nose and I frowned in annoyance. He was exceptional at finding me. It seemed the more time he monitored me the more he became attuned to my scent. I lifted myself from the ground. The mother boar looked at me, unfazed. I smiled at her briefly before I began walking into the other direction. When I got further away from the little boars I began to run so I would not startle them. Ara ran alongside me, forcing a great smile on my face; we were always so happy to run together. As I anticipated, Trim's pace quickened as mine did, and he began to give chase.

I ran past the great waterfall I often enjoyed while basking in my own thoughts. I ran through the mist and broke through some trees into an open field of deer. They were not scared to see me there as I had always run with them. They never feared my presence as I did not hunt them. It was nice to simply run and keep with their pace. As I looked back, I began to laugh as Trim ran behind me.

I ran with the deer, hiding amongst them. My smile vanished as unfamiliar scents swarmed my senses and a loud, screeching noise pierced the air. One of the deer dropped to the ground. My canines bit deeply into my lip as I ran for the young doe, standing over her in horror. An arrow had pierced into her chest but she was not yet dead. My eyes widened and my mouth stretched savagely. I looked for those who did this and saw that they were approaching me on horse. Ara began growling as I did.

The deer frantically ran away from their attackers. They streamed around me as I crouched, hiding so I could observe the enemy. There were eight of them. All of their pack had a light-gray fur with bronze-colored skin. They were now close and I rose to my feet just as the archer raised his bow again. I leapt for him, ripping the bow and arrow from his hands. I paused to evaluate the closest and strongest scent, and when I found it, I jumped on him, throwing him off his horse. I slammed him viciously into the ground. My body steadied over his, pinning him down as I arched the arrow under his neck.

The other horses were startled by my quick actions and the two closest were pulled back so they did not trample the strong male I held below me. He was of my age. His pale-brown eyes looked back at me, surprised but not frightened. His hair was long and it trailed over his hard chest. His frame was not overly big but still impressive. As I took another whiff of his unfamiliar scent I realized he was not the Alpha. I turned, snarling, to those who surrounded me.

My eyes narrowed on the Alpha. He had rough facial fur and his nose seemed to have been broken far too many times. And as I sniffed again I understood the one I had pinned to be his son, as well as another who sat next to the father. The brother had shorter hair and much broader shoulders. I judged him to be older than the brother I had attacked by about ten years. All of this pack had the same shimmery, bronzed skin from too much time spent in the sun.

"Who are you to trespass on my land and hunt on my grounds?" I snarled, edging the arrow into the young wolf's throat when he tried to raise himself from the ground.

"Who are *we*?" the Alpha repeated in indignation. His tone was hollow and his eyes were devoid of emotion.

"You are to lower your weapons!" Trim commanded to the foreigners. He ran to my side, standing in front of me protectively.

The Alpha raised his impressive sword in front of Trim. "And what kind of beast are you?" he snarled contemptuously.

I snarled viciously, pulling the wolf I held captive to his feet. I tugged him toward his father with the arrow still at his throat. "You will not speak to my wolves like that!" I said with authority, my canines digging into my bottom lip.

"Sia, it is okay," Trim said lightly under his breath. The insult to Trim's appearance apparently infuriated me more so than him.

"I will have you all killed if you say one more disrespectful thing on my land toward my pack members. I will begin with your son." I emphasized my words by pulling on his hair so that his throat was even more exposed to my weapon.

"Really, Fimble, you have yourself attacked and held at ransom by a woman. You never cease to amaze me," the older brother chuckled, evidently taking my threat lightly.

I gasped in disbelief at Trim's speed as he tore his sword out and jumped onto the older brother, slamming him to the ground. His sword was instantly held at the wolf's throat. The last archer raised his bow and arrow to Trim's back.

Trim snarled into the wolf's face, "You will not speak to Princess Sia in such a way, you piece of rotten flesh." His nails dug into the man's shoulder as he held him down.

"Men, stand down," the Alpha commanded instantly, now looking at me in a different light. "Well, my apologies, Princess Sia.

We did not know we were to be escorted to the castle grounds. We simply hunted for gifts to present to you upon our arrival."

I stopped baring my fangs as I realized the mistake I had made. "Kratin?" I said slowly, embarrassed that I hadn't thought of it sooner. My mother and father would be so unhappy to hear I had savagely attacked our guests. And yet my mistrust for them stopped me from releasing my grip on the younger brother's light-gray fur.

"I am most apologetic. I should have identified you sooner as the princess with your radiant black fur, how embarrassing of me to think you feral," he said with nonchalance.

Trim retracted his sword from the older brother's throat and walked toward me. The wolf angrily stood up, embarrassed at being dominated by Trim.

"But, the consequences of *your* actions, young man, are of some interest to me. How will the King and Queen react to one of their subjects mistreating their guests?" Kratin taunted Trim.

"Nowhere near as angrily, I imagine, as how they will react when they see that these guests have left a bleeding wound on their only daughter, kind sir," Trim replied calmly. Both Kratin and I looked down to the small graze on my arm that bled only slightly. I hadn't even noticed it. I looked at Trim in disbelief, surprised that he would notice such a small cut on me.

"My apologies, my lady," Kratin said, dismounting his horse and dropping to his knee.

"She is not *your* lady," Trim spat angrily.

Kratin looked at him with an insincere smile, and then looked to the ground, as if hiding his expression. "Well, not yet."

There was an awkward silence. The chilled air brushed through us, sweeping my braided fringe past my eyes. I struggled to find the words to end the conversation.

"For goodness sake, Father. We have amended our wrong, now have her let go of Fimble," a woman's voice spoke out from the back of the pack. The pack parted at her voice and we watched as a wolf with gray hair, bronze skin, and light-brown eyes that were framed by impossibly thick eyelashes jumped down from her horse and walked toward us. Her legs were far longer than mine and her appearance was radiant. I had no doubt that she would be admired as a magnificent wolf by all who seen her.

"I am Fiesca," she said coolly, looking down at me. Her bountiful chest was at my eyelevel. I bit on my lip, jealous of her height. "Please let my brother go." Although her tone was polite and clipped, there was an order behind her words, not a request.

Trim stood closer to me. Still I could not let go of the wolf; I was surprised by my own hesitance.

"Sia," Trim whispered gently, brushing his fingers across my forearm before pulling at the arrow in my hand. I slowly loosened my grip on the younger brother's fur and his light-gray ears pulled back in pain.

"My apologies," I said, stumbling into Trim awkwardly. I felt dazed by the situation. I looked down at Ara, who looked to me before growling at the woman. Fiesca's brown eyes contemplated my little fox in distaste.

"Please do not apologize, Princess Sia, it was my fault for giving consent to hunt on your land. I can see that is much to your personal distaste," Fimble said, bowing to me. His hand was across his chest, and he seemed gentlemanly in appearance. His long light-gray hair reached to his hips and he looked at me with earnest eyes and a small smile. "I do hope you can forgive us and welcome us by escorting us to your castle?"

"Of course," I said, taken aback by the mannerly disposition that was so unlike that of the rest of his pack. The smell of blood lingered on my nose and I looked back over at the doe that had been struck. It still gasped for breath. "Please excuse me for a moment," I pardoned myself, catching Fiesca's eye. I turned away from the woman who intimidated me with her long legs and luscious curves.

As I walked toward the doe, I winced as if its pain were my own. It was a young deer. When we hunted on our land we were to only aim for the elderly who had lived their life fruitfully. We tried not to take more lives than we needed to sustain ourselves. My father gave consent to this request when I was of a young age. My eyes always filled with tears to see so many beasts hunted before my eyes. The beasts sensed my compassion and allowed me to stay close and run with them. It was as if somehow they knew me to be no threat, no matter what my nature may be biologically.

Trim walked protectively behind me, on guard after our confrontation. I dropped to my knees beside the young doe, gliding my hand over her nose and soothing her. I reached for the arrow and put her out of her misery. She squealed softly before her breath against my hand ceased. I looked to the blue sky, apologetic that she had been killed too soon. I gave thanks to her for the food that would feed my pack. I turned to Trim, grateful for his presence. "I neither like them nor trust them," I spoke honestly.

"If you need me, you know I will be close," Trim said, offering his hand to me to help me stand. I looked back over at the pack which we were to now escort to my castle. I thanked Trim for the help, wanting so much to continue holding his hand as I tentatively approached the pack again. I felt the pressure of my parents request that I be respectful and well-mannered. Trim's hand dropped from mine and I squared my shoulders. How desperate could my father be to align with such a pack?

Chapter Four- Comparison of Two

Walking alongside Trim and Ara, I couldn't help but feel agitated by the pack. I eyed the horses that they rode. Horses should be wild and free, not mounted and treated as though they were beneath our kind. From the corner of my eye I watched the long-legged wolf named Fiesca. Her body jolted slowly up and down as her horse moved beneath her. She looked spitefully over the trees and the small animals that hid from us as if our land were not to her liking.

Trim cautiously watched them as well, creating distance between them and me by walking between us. It was nice to have such protection. As much as I believed I could look after myself, the Alpha, eldest son and daughter made me uncomfortable. The younger brother, Fimble, seemed gentlemanly enough to be pardoned for the feral manners the others carried. *Is all of their pack members like this? I wonder how their territory looks, and how they care for the animals that live there?*

We led them back through the forest but took them a longer way on a small trail instead of by the waterfall I admired so much. That was my haven and special sanctuary; I hated to think others might occupy that same space. The sun shined brightly from above, allowing patches of brightness to seep through the thick foliage above us as the trees and vines swayed lightly in the breeze.

It was almost peaceful walking through the trees. Many of the smaller animals hid from our visitors. As we approached the open space before my castle's walls, I began to feel uneasy, recalling how I had lied to Hansel. I looked back at Trim regretfully as Hansel ran for me from the gates. Trim had no sympathy in his eye for me as it was not the first time I had done this. Usually by now he would have scolded me for misbehaving once again. If we didn't have guests I imagined he would say, "Well, if only you hadn't escaped the castle walls once again..."

"Princess Sia!" Hansel huffed as he came to a stop in front of me. As he took in the guests behind us he began to flex his strong, muscular arms and smooth back his hair. "You promised me you would not leave my side!"

It's because of the bountiful wolf behind me that he flexed, I thought to myself contemptuously.

"You left me very frightened for your safety!" he exaggerated, kneeling and grabbing my hand to kiss it. Trim grabbed my hand back, shooting Hansel an unimpressed look. Often Trim had to shield me from Hansel's flirtatious gestures as he knew how much it had annoyed me from a young age. But now it seemed it was not only me it annoyed, but Trim also. Hansel's dramatics bored me but he was usually like this. It surprised me to see such a vicious expression on Trim. *I thought it was only me that received those looks. Does he scorn everyone?* I thought, trying to contain my small smile. He treated everyone like a child, even a man his own size.

"I took Princess Sia for the outing that she requested. But this is not the time to discuss her timetable," Trim said challengingly. Hansel looked at the ground, as if biting his tongue on words he should not say, before looking back to Trim.

I placed both my hands over theirs, grabbing their attention before giving them a bright smile. It was an act in front of our guests; my parents told me to be on my best behavior. "I thank you both. Shall we lead our *guests* into the castle?" I said, highlighting "guests" so that they would remember we were not alone. Even if I did not like this pack, we could not appear as dysfunctional in front of them before they had even reached our gates. Trim and Hansel were two of our highest ranked warriors.

43

And right now they seemed cubbish. We had to prove to rival packs that if for any reason they wanted to challenge us for the Kingdom then we could protect ourselves. We could not let outsiders see there were rivalries or weak spots within.

Hansel smiled at the guests charismatically and clapped his hands together. His performance made me cringe as this was not a pack that wanted to play audience to his theatrics. Trim walked toward the castle, oblivious to my stare. I looked at him, confused. Usually he held the highest respect for formalities. And yet, he had slightly slipped today. *Does Hansel rattle him that much, or is he worried about this unfamiliar pack?*

"Right this way, please," I instructed politely, hiding the bitterness I felt toward them. Kratin kicked his horse in the stomach to indicate for it to go forward. I had to clench my fists firmly to my sides to stop myself from reaching out to the poor creature in dismay.

As we walked through the entrance of our castle walls, I looked amongst the huts. Cubs hid behind their siblings, peeking out at the new pack. One little cub had his ears pulled back—he smelled the scent and sneezed at it. I couldn't help but smile at the accuracy of his judgment. I too thought them an unsavory pack. Women held rags and animal pelts that had been hanging out to dry in the sun close to their chest in discomfort as they too watched us pass.

Siesta ran from the castle, meeting us amongst the huts. I glanced in the direction of Lady Momiko's hut where I had escaped from only hours ago. I sighed heavily. *I am yet again at my starting point, back within the castle walls like a good princess...*

"Lady Sia, Princess Momiko has requested to see you," Siesta said, curtsying to the pack behind me. Fimble gave her a bright smile as the others rudely looked around at our people as if they were beneath them.

"Lady Momiko, she is the wolf who uses moonstone and can connect with Spirit Packs, is she not?" Fimble asked inquisitively, dismounting his horse and greeting Siesta formerly.

"You know of Lady Momiko?" I asked surprised. Trim had always taught me that it should not be of great interest to another pack about their surrounding packs. Usually the only reason another would enquire or try to gain intelligence about another pack was if they were interested in gaining their territory.

"Well of course the stories are well-known since the days of the third Phantom Wolf," Fimble's brother announced over him. "Lady Momiko helped kill the past king, your uncle, if I recall the stories accurately? To hear that such a woman is now accepted within the very same castle walls has generated great intrigue."

Trim and I both stood still; it was as hard for me as it was for him to keep our mouths closed against the reproachful words we wanted to spit in his face. My uncle Taleb was a terrible man. It was he who befriended that human, Thomas, who was responsible for the death of Sia and her pack. Thomas was the human who had turned Sia into a Phantom Wolf. My mother only had dark words to speak of Taleb for all he had done to her dear friend Sia. The Kingdom was tainted after he killed his own parents to claim kingship. He even had my other uncle Kiba turned into a Phantom Wolf. Taleb directed for his own brother to be cursed as a Phantom Wolf. My own mother and father would have been slaughtered. A human who kills a wolf is forever connected to them, cursing them in a state of life and death as a Phantom Wolf. If Thomas hadn't already slaughtered her pack before cursing her, Sia would have been fated to kill them with her bare hands.

It was Sia who was forced to stop him, as my mother, father, Lady Momiko, and Trim watched. I looked at Trim as I thought of this. He would have watched Sia kill her lover—my Uncle Kiba— as somehow they were both turned into Phantom

45

Wolves. Lady Momiko had once suggested to my mother that it was their spiritual connection that tied them rather than an earthly entwinement.

That was the day after Trim had his face clawed when protecting Sia from one of the warriors that Taleb had sent to kill her. Trim protected her, but due to infection and further difficulties with his eye, he had lost its sight and then lost it completely. Lady Momiko explained that it was not his eye he was terrified to lose, but Sia. He mourned her and was tortured by the fact that he did not properly say goodbye. As a young cub he had wished her farewell without knowing they would be separated by her death.

Lady Momiko nursed him through his pain and his childhood. She was like a mother to him, and to have her name so tainted, especially in her current state of illness, was disgraceful. Many were in favor of the changeover of kingship and only a few retreated with Taleb's body after Sia attacked and killed both him and the human, Thomas. But by killing Thomas her life was taken as well because of the curse—thus the cruel bond between a human and his Phantom Wolf. She was to live in a state of immortality until his death, but by killing him she chose to take her own life as well for all he had done to her family and her love, Kiba.

Lady Momiko fell ill and began to realize she had Spirit Pack sight and could speak to those who had passed. She could even see glimpses of the future. Using her gift she had seen the horrific night when Sia was cursed and her pack slaughtered. And since Trim's birth, she was guided by her premonition to believe that Sia was fated to meet him. She also knew Trim was meant for greatness—in my eyes he was already great. Lady Momiko whispered it into my ears as a young cub, told me the stories that my mother and father were hesitant to tell. She made me promise never to tell him.

After many packs had been torn apart over the hunt for Sia, the third Phantom Wolf, the Kingdom was slowly built on the foundations of my parents' aim: for all packs to no longer fear the humans; to no longer segregate and be territorial; to come together as an entity and under the one kingdom. But still, packs fought in fear that the humans would come.

My eyes bored into the eyes of the foreign, repulsive wolf. The wind quickened its pace and whipped my black braided fringe in front of my eyes. Once again I was unsure how to answer.

"Lish, that was disrespectful," Fimble said angrily after a heavy silence. "It is not because of malicious gossip that we are here. We have heard of her greatness in foretelling the future and seeing things. Her ability to communicate with Spirit Packs is awfully intriguing. I would like to meet her myself."

"Only Princess Sia has been called upon," Trim said sternly, standing over me. Fimble was only a little taller than me. Trim's height even intimidated me sometimes.

Not many knew of Lady Momiko's recent illness, and it was to be kept a secret, especially from a pack that we knew nothing of. It was particularly suspicious to me that they should take a special interest in Lady Momiko's gift. For them to meet her and find her in such a vulnerable state was not a chance we could take, especially when we did not know yet if they harbored peaceful or hostile intentions. It seemed odd to me that my father would welcome such an intimidating pack into our castle. Was this alliance something he needed so greatly?

"Of course, please pardon my intrusion," Fimble said with a faint smile. Fimble seemed different to his pack; they were harsh and barbaric. Even the two archers who were not his immediate family looked down on my fellow pack with a guarded interest. Fimble seemed gentle and when I looked into his light-brown eyes, I could not see the same wildness. "Please do take your leave. I am sure Trim here can lead us to the King and Queen."

"Thank you," I said courteously. I could not glare at him as harshly as I did the others. I already felt guilty for threatening his life only minutes ago.

I glanced at Trim. He watched me calculatingly from where he stood before the path to the garden. We used to play there so happily until his heart grew cold. We had spent much time together. All my life he had been here with me—chasing, teaching, protecting me. When he looked at me so distantly I did not know what he was thinking. His heart closed off to all those around him, except for Lady Momiko. But as he grew older they drifted apart and they exchanged less and less words.

"Siesta, please guide our guests to comfort."

"Of course, Princess," Siesta said, curtseying next to Trim as I walked ahead. Ara barked at me, grabbing my attention. She looked up at me with large eyes of concern. She was always sensitive to my emotions and always knew when something troubled me. I stopped and patted my chest lightly to permit her to jump up. As she did I caught her and bundled her tightly to my chest for comfort.

"Princess Sia?" Fimble spoke from behind me. I had not yet reached the doors and looked back at him. His pack dismounted their horses, allowing my guards to lead them away. They patted over their bodies as if dirty. "Will I be seeing you tonight at dinner?"

My eyes involuntarily diverted to Trim, who continued looking straight ahead. Red blushed across my cheeks and I looked down, embarrassed that I had looked at him in such a way. I knew he would not look at me, even after the heated moment we had shared during training. He had no interest in me, no matter how deeply I desired it. I felt foolish for looking at him with such an exposed expression. Was I after his permission? Was I hoping for his disapproval?

"Yes," I said quietly, still hiding my face behind my black fringe before turning and walking into the castle. I started past the Great Hall, where we were soon to dine. I walked faster than usual, as if running from the situation. Stroking Ara in my arms, I felt foolish for letting my guard down in such a way.

My heart patted at the forwardness of Fimble, who I now noticed to be very handsome. He seemed the opposite of Trim— gentle and open with his words and thoughts. I felt ashamed of having such an immature heart when it came to love when I thought of myself as a strong-minded and determined woman.

I quickly paced past the library in case my mother for any reason may have still been in there. But by now my parents should have been notified of our guests. I clutched Ara even closer to my chest. I dreaded a lecture over how I had first greeted them. I walked down a long, narrow hallway that had numerous paintings of my pack and the generations that preceded them. I greeted a few of the wolves who regularly cleaned and walked toward the bathing chambers on the left. On my right was a long hall which was lit by flamed torches on the wall. I turned toward the first door on my right. Hesitantly I reached out for the knob, unsure as to why Lady Momiko had summoned me. Like a cub, I was pleased I could see her and that she had requested for me to come.

"Stop your hesitation," Lady Momiko's stern voice echoed through the door. Her cough quickly subsided and she continued, "I'm not getting any younger."

Chapter Five- To be Equals

The room was very dark and smelled of decay. There were animal pelts covering the window, darkening the few strips of light that peeked through. There was not much in this room, only a seat in the corner of the room and a small wooden table. The stew on the table had gone cold and it no longer smelled appetizing.

I looked over Lady Momiko, saddened. She had slightly raised herself in the bed. It was covered with dark rags and animal pelts that contrasted with her ghostly-white skin and gray eyes. The heavy knowledge of what was soon to come hung in the air. It pained me to see her struggle to stay with us. Those who took care of Lady Momiko recently noticed that she did not wish to eat much and that she spent a lot of time sleeping. Her youth still radiated in her green eyes and it was only the fragility of her body that exhibited her illness. For all the gray fur and sagged skin, you knew by her eyes she had lived a very long, fulfilling life.

"Do not look at me as if I were already dead," Lady Momiko's voice sounded crisp, and yet it still held an element of humor. I was only grateful the stick she often carried around with her was not so close to her bed. Often when I was younger she would hit me on the head with it—sometimes for lying, sometimes for mocking or even just for a scornful look that insinuated I was biting back some smart comment. She would clobber me, order me to respect my elders and upbraid me for souring my pretty face with insolent looks.

"How do you feel?" I asked, lowering myself gently onto the edge of her bed. I looked deeply into her dim green eyes. As I asked she let a large cough out, spluttering against her hand and then holding her hand to her chest.

"Like far too many people are making an ordeal over my bag of bones," she replied with a tart smile, straightening her back against the wall. "How do you fare, my young one?"

"In what respect?" I asked, straightening out one of the rags and tucking her in more tightly.

"I hear that another pack has taken interest in your beauty, and your father is using you as bait, so to speak."

I smiled lightly, Lady Momiko was always forward with her words. She knew how much it antagonized me that people only spoke of my appearance, not the traits or strengths I had to offer my pack.

"Like a piece of meat," I said sharply. "I do not know why father wishes to align himself with such a pack. They are rude and obnoxious, although the youngest brother, Fimble, speaks kindly and has commendable manners. I cannot understand what my father is planning and why, even now when I am almost of eighteen years of age, he wishes to keep me separate from politics. Perhaps if he explained and let me understand some of the actions he takes, I could properly present myself. I am not as foolish as they treat me."

"My dear, sweet one, sometimes ignorance is bliss. Your father does not wish to burden you with these worries. He still sees you as his only cub. I am sure he does not wish to worry you with these things until you are of an age of entwinement and are near ready to take his place," she soothed, before coughing harshly.

"I am just tired of being treated as that—a princess and a cub. For so long now I have tried to show myself as a strong wolf in front of my peers but all they wish to do is comb my hair and treat me like a flower. I am drowning in the nurturing they give," I said looking down at my thick black hair. I was only ever 'pretty' to them—the words became an insult to me from a young age. I did not want to become vain. I wanted to fight amongst my kind and yet even my training was treated like a magic trick.

"Is it they who give you too much attention, or a certain someone who gives you too little?" she probed, her eyebrows rising as she looked at me with mischief in her eyes. I knew her question was rhetorical and that she had Trim in mind. She was the only person in my pack I could not hide my affection from, perhaps because she was gifted enough to see it. "They nurture you so because your curiosity always takes you away from their protection, outside of the castle walls."

"I do not wish to be followed. And it is you who encouraged me to do so!" I said, surprised she would lecture me about it when it was her who had helped me so many times to escape. It was because of this and her unique nurturing that I could find myself, and run wildly with the animals—that felt so right within my blood. The thrill of the unknown tempted my curious nature.

"I lost my curiosity a long time ago," she said with a small smile, looking at me evenly. She needn't even say it. I understood why. She had for half her lifetime now been able to see predictions of the future, how could she possibly be curious when everything was already known to her? Did she let me be swept over by my own curiosity because she was regretful that she could not do the same?

"Do you think it will make me less of a queen one day?" I asked. I know a lot of wolves saw it as immature that I escaped so often, but I couldn't deny myself the thrill of being outside the walls. I often wondered if the wolves would consider me unreliable and too silly to rule. *Do they think I will abandon them because I believe there is more elsewhere?*

"I think it is what will make you a *great* queen," she reassured me with a bright smile. "I have seen it."

52

"Can you tell me more?" I said leaning toward her eagerly. My ears speedily pinned back and I jarred upright as she looked at me with an angry face. She told very few of what she saw unless she deemed it necessary, but most of her knowledge she kept to herself.

"I have told you many times. If one can see the future, they should not speak of what they see; I mean this, Sia. Please remember this. It can change one's complete outlook on life. You cannot change what is being shown. The knowledge of that alone can ruin a wolf's mentality and their outlook on life. You cannot tell someone what it is they are meant to experience."

There was an awkward silence between us as I contemplated her words. She had always stressed this message.

"If you could see the future, or speak to your Spirit Pack, how do you think that would influence your life?" she asked seriously. I was surprised by her question, and began to wonder why she had summoned me to her room.

"I don't know," I answered honestly. Never had I even thought of being in Lady Momiko's position. *I wonder if she has already seen what will happen to all of us once she passes? I wonder if it is tiring to be able to call on the deceased of our pack? I wonder if it is joyful? Can she do it at any time? Is she thankful to have such a gift?* But she could only speak with *her* Spirit Pack she once explained to me. She and I were not of the same pack, although under the same kingdom.

"My little one," she said, reaching for my hand. As she turned her hand over she revealed her blue moonstone, the one which she favored most. She gently placed it in my hands and closed my fingers over it. "This is the first of three gifts I will bestow upon you for the celebration of your birth; it has now been eighteen years. I am tired, and I am dying. If ever you feel lonely or feel as if you need my guidance, call for me. Talk to me, keep this stone close. I will be near," she promised quietly.

I looked down at the blue moonstone. Most of these stones we filed so that they were smooth enough to be worn around our necks, ears, and hips for great feasts. Lady Momiko had wanted hers to stay with its flaws and imperfections. A tear slid down my eye as I looked down at the blue moonstone, understanding its significance. This was the moonstone Lady Momiko often used when she were speaking with her Spirit Pack. All my life she had been educating me on such things— of how connectivity was most possible at a full moon, for example. I grappled with her meaning. Did she no longer intend on speaking with her Spirit Pack? For so long I had believed Lady Momiko would fight this illness but now with this gift it seemed she was facing her death.

I looked up at her questioningly but she only smiled back casually before looking over at her stick. "Can you please reach that for me?" Hesitantly I walked over to the stick, lifting it and then handing it to her carefully. Although a thin stick, it was weighty. The golden bells on it jingled as it shifted.

"I want you to have this too," she said after a moment's hesitation.

"I cannot accept this as well, Lady Momiko, do you not wish anything to be buried with you? Would you not give this to Trim, at least?"

"What do I need a stick for when I am dead?" she snapped. "I have given Trim what I believe he needs, and the same goes for you. If you ever need help walking or cannot lift yourself to see the sight of day, just look at this and find the strength within it to do so."

"You speak in riddles, Lady Momiko, I do not understand." As swiftly as always the stick smacked me on my head and I winced. I rubbed my head; it had been a while since she had smacked me so.

"I do not speak in riddles. I am just old," she said with yet another knowing smile. She pushed the stick toward me. Why would she give these items to me? I wondered why Trim did not want them. I thought Trim and Lady Momiko were closer than what she and I were. She had been like a second mother to Trim so I was hesitant to receive such valuable gifts.

"Do look after my Trim in my absence," she said earnestly. Her eyes looked wet and yet she seemed happy. She did not fear death, but I had hoped she would survive for another year at least.

"I don't think he will let me," I laughed as I brushed away a few tears. She laughed with me, as we both knew how closed Trim was and how very little help he needed from others.

"Now go, I am tired," she said, slowly lowering herself beneath the furs once again. I slightly tucked her in, pushing away her thin wiry gray hair from her forehead. Her fever still grew. I gently kissed her on the forehead in goodbye. I could not convey my gratitude for the life we had spent together and all that she had taught me throughout.

"Please do look over us," I whispered gently before leaving the room with the moonstone and her stick in my hands. I hesitated at the door, counting that there were only two gifts instead of three. As I looked back at her panting face, I dismissed it due to her old age. *Has she already slipped this far?*

I paused on the outside of the door for a moment, enjoying the fresh, cool breeze that swept through the castle. It was nice to have some time alone. Ara sat quietly next to me. She had waited for me the whole time outside of the room. I swallowed my sadness about Lady Momiko. Like she said, I will still speak to her, even if she could no longer hear or give advice back. I would always turn to her when I was in need.

Walking down the hall toward the library I greeted the same wolves who were earlier in the bathing chambers. Kratin's deep, monstrous laugh echoed through the walls, scratching at my ears. I glanced into the Great Hall where we would feast later and saw that Trim was watching me from the corner of his eye as he stood tall behind Fimble and the others. Fimble also noticed me. He gave me a small wave before diverting his attention back to where my parents were seated. My mother and father were welcoming their guests most humbly to our territory. Trim's eye followed me sharply before he slowly looked back toward my father. Slightly antagonized by his watchful gaze, I walked back toward my room. It was still a few hours before our feast would be prepared and if I hid in my room I would not have to put myself in such an awkward position as to pretend to enjoy the company of *that* pack.

I continued down the hallway but within seconds I knew I was no longer alone. The flames that flickered on the walls projected the shadow of his tail swishing back and forth. Trim's overpowering scent followed me. I recalled the night before when he had promised he would not leave my side. I did not dare to turn around and look at him. His harsh stare was imprinted in my mind. He had always been like this, nothing had changed, and yet it infuriated me every time. Why could he not look at me with the kindness I so desperately wanted from him?

Ara growled at him from behind, warning him to stay back. It was not that she didn't like Trim—in fact, she hated most males—but she usually enjoyed Trim's company. Because of my agitated vibe she warned him off until we were both within my room. I slammed the door behind me and sat on my animal pelts, looking at the gifts Lady Momiko bestowed on me. I tightened my grip around her stick, questioning how she wanted me to look after Trim—her dying wish—if he would not even see me as an equal.

Chapter Six- Red Rose

$\mathcal{I}$ spent hours dwelling on Lady Momiko and what would happen to her. I wondered who amongst the villagers knew of the severity of her illness. The gravity of the situation weighed heavily upon my shoulders. It was Lady Momiko who wanted her illness to be kept quiet, but I felt as if I were cheating the villagers out of the chance to say goodbye.

Trim said nothing but remained quietly by my door. The aroma of his scent annoyed me. Questions taunted me. *Is he keeping an eye on me at all times because I might leave the castle walls again? Or is it because of the new pack that preoccupies my parents beneath us? Why must he stay so close?*

"Princess? I am coming in," Siesta's kind voice cut into my thoughts. She opened the door without waiting for a reply, so I covered my face and looked toward the window. I did not want Trim to catch a glimpse of me in such a distressed state. I needed to prove to him I was strong and that I could handle things. But all I wanted to do was nestle into his hard chest and cry. He would miss Lady Momiko greatly and I wondered if he had or would ever shed a tear for her. Perhaps Sia, the Phantom Wolf, was the only one for whom he would cry.

"You are filthy, still!" she exclaimed. "We must go to the bathing chambers straight away. I cannot very well present you in front of the King and Queen like this."

"I do not wish to bathe. I will do so after dinner," I said, dismissing her.

"I think not! You still have blood on your hands," Siesta said, grabbing my hands and holding them out. As she did so she revealed Lady Momiko's blue moonstone in my hand. She paused for a moment, clearly understanding the sentimental value it held for me. When her bright eyes met mine I saw sympathy. I rolled my fingers over it once again gently and looked down at my body. Siesta was right, I was still dirty and had blood on my hands from the morning's events.

I lifted Ara off the bed gently, who whined as she woke. I placed Lady Momiko's stick against my bed and the moonstone on my table. "You are right, we must quickly bathe," I conceded, already regretting my harshness. It was not Siesta's fault that I was in such a foul mood. Siesta walked briskly ahead to open the door for me and instantly my eyes fell on Trim's lurking shadow. He glanced at my red eyes quickly before looking away and taking his position behind me.

We walked toward the bathing chambers in uncomfortable silence. "Truly, to the bathing chambers as well?" I turned suddenly and snapped at him. I was deeply unhappy with his sudden eagerness to follow me everywhere. He left the reasons for his actions unsaid and made me feel even more distant from him, despite his proximity. He opened his mouth, the expression on his face a clear indication that he was mustering some cutting remark, but suddenly he seemed to fall short of words. I turned from him, wondering what it was that had captivated his attention over my shoulder.

Fiesca was standing in front of me. The flickering of the flames in the darkened hallway cast shadows over her womanly shape. "Have you not yet prepared yourself for the feast?" she said. She walked toward me purposefully and I knew she was enjoying how the flames appeared to caress her curvaceous figure. Her hips swayed far too much for my liking. Her seductive smile irritated me too, but the eyes that looked at Trim hungrily were even worse. "It appears you're still filthy from attacking my brother... like a beast."

"Princess Sia is not like that, my lady," Siesta countered, quickly jumping to my defense. Her eyes fell to the ground under Fiesca's scrutinizing glare.

"Do you honestly dare speak back to me, cub?" she smirked, her light-brown eyes appraising Siesta.

"You will not speak to her or anyone else here in that manner. If you do, I will deal with you personally," I threatened, no longer able to contain my anger. I disliked the woman but I also pitied her for the animosity that gleamed in her eye—she was obviously consumed by hatred. She stepped forward once again, her chest at my eyelevel. She looked down over me in an intimidating manner.

"That, little Princess, I would like to see," she said, her canines showing as her plump pink lips stretched into a mocking smile. Even her skin had a shimmery, bronze glow in the flicker of the flames. It angered me that such beauty contained such evil within. *Is this the cost of such good looks?*

I went to step forward, more than happy to accept her challenge, but Trim's hand reached out for my arm, stopping me. Fiesca also noticed and mirrored my disappointment. Trim did not break eye contact with her as he clamped down on my skin. I looked up imploringly but he did not return my stare. All I could see was a calm determination in his eye, the other side of his face obscured by shadows.

They stared at one another, caught in a silent struggle for dominancy over the situation. Trim held me back so tightly it took my breath away. No matter how much I wanted to force her to take her words back, I knew it was futile as I would have to fight through Trim first. A sound echoed through the empty hallway and we all listened, suddenly alert. Fiesca's ears pulled back; it was Fimble calling her name from afar.

"Well, I feel as if it's my time to depart. But I do look forward to our dance," she said, her eyes lingering on Trim. Her look now was full of promise— no longer domineering, but flirtatious. I glanced up quickly and to my relief he held the same stern expression he always had.

We watched her leave in silence. I tutted in exasperation as I folded my arms. "I would have been fine," I said to him, annoyed that he had doubted my abilities.

"You cannot. Your father has called them here. Do you not think there is reason for that? Do you think he called them here so you could challenge them to a fight?"

"I do not need you to look after me," I said angrily, my canine biting into my lip.

"Then who will keep you out of trouble?" he demanded.

The candles on the walls flickered as a cool breeze swept past us. I shivered as the chill lingered on my skin. The shadows flickered back and forth over his face. I looked into his eye and read the exhaustion there. He was watching over me at the expense of his own sleep. I noticed our closeness in the hallway. Because of how heated our words had become we had both taken steps close enough to inhale one another's words. I looked into his beautiful blue eye, unsure of what to say. My heart raced at our closeness, which only infuriated me more.

"I do not need you to," I said again calmly, pulling away from him. I didn't need to be treated as a cub. I did not need him chasing me, no matter how wonderful and fun it may have seemed in the past when I was younger. I did not need him as my strength because I had my own, even if he would not acknowledge it. My heart has already grown too attached to the fantasy of him being by my side forever. But one day he would entwine with another, and it would not be me. Perhaps it would be a wolf such as Fiesca—someone tall, bountiful, and beautiful.

I pulled away from him, no longer allowing myself to be consumed by him. I had been foolish for so long. Trim only ever pulled me back from anything that challenged me in life. He claimed his protectiveness was for my own good, but it stunted my growth. I could not suffer his stifling presence any longer just so I could have him near. If he didn't want me, then I would not have him so close by. Siesta shifted uncomfortably, reminding me suddenly of her and Ara's presence.

"Leave me," I said quietly to him.

"No," he answered, looking past me and avoiding my eyes.

"I said, *leave*." My voice shook with emotion but the authority of my tone startled him and he looked quickly into my eyes. I noticed my vision of him blur and I lowered my head, suddenly exhausted. *I cannot let him see me cry.*

Siesta stepped forward calmly, taking control of the situation. "Please, Trim," she said quietly. She held my shoulders firmly and I relaxed under her motherly grip. "Princess Sia has been through a small ordeal today. I think it best that I console her in the way only a woman can."

I wanted to hide in Siesta's warmth, grateful that she would stand up for me in such a way with both Trim and Fiesca. To my astonishment he listened to Siesta and left us alone. I held my breath as I listened to his footsteps die away. I felt pathetic that I couldn't keep myself together. After a few deep breaths I patted Siesta's hand to let her know I was okay and now calm. "Thank you, Siesta, for everything," I said, reflecting on her braveness. Siesta was not a warrior in any sense and it warmed me to know she would defend me. She had looked after me for many years now and never had she once complained. I was very grateful to have her by my side. Especially at a time like this when I felt as if I had no one.

We walked quietly together to the bathing chambers. I hesitated to walk past the room that contained Lady Momiko. Turning into the large bathing chambers, steam assaulted my senses from the hot water. We had another two bathing chambers next to this one so guests and other wolves could gain access to the hot water at any time. Two wolves poked a small fire under a tub of hot water. I quickly walked up a few steps and lowered myself gratefully into the bath. Surrounding me were reflections of myself as large mirrors spread over the walls. As I looked ahead of me I could see the half-moon trying to shine through the gray clouds. There was an open space in the wall allowing bathers to look out at the stars. One of our royal ancestors had requested the hole. He announced that he wanted to enjoy the view every night when he came to bathe. And he was right. As I felt my body cleanse, it was as if my mind did as well under the night sky.

I washed over my pale skin while examining my freckles. Siesta scrubbed vigorously at my hair. Usually we would speak about the day's events or gossip about wolves entwining or giving birth. But today we sat quietly. I gazed into the half lit sky. I wanted this silence; I simply wanted to *be.* I dreaded my next encounter with *that* pack once again.

I thought over Trim's words. I tried to understand my father's intentions. Of course I didn't mean to challenge his guests. I knew he had his reasons; I only wanted to be respected enough to be included in the discussions about them. I sank further into the water, hiding half my face. Only my eyes broke through the surface of the water. *Why do Mother and Father still conceal these things from me? Am I a disappointment to them? Do they not trust me?* I rolled my eyes in agitation, annoyed that I was always torturing myself with such questions. Siesta tipped a bucket of water over my newly washed hair before handing me a rag to dry myself.

I stepped out of the bath and shivered in the night air. Looking into the reflection of the mirror next to me, I questioned what my face would look like if it were somehow different. My hair was free from braids and cascaded past my shoulders in a mass of waves. *What if my hair wasn't so thick and black? What if I didn't have freckles and my eyes were not so large and blue? What if my chest was ample and I had hips instead of a small stomach and legs...* I looked away from the mirror, disappointed in my own insecurities. It seemed the more people called me beautiful the more I doubted it myself. And although many labelled me exquisite, there was only one whom I wanted to see me in that way. I touched my rose-red lips absentmindedly, thinking of the flowers in the garden. I fantasized that one day Trim would offer me one.

"Princess Sia?" Siesta waved her hand in front of me. I looked at her in embarrassment. I had dazed off into my own fantasy world.

"Apologies," I said quickly, sitting before her. She combed through my hair and neatly tidied it into a bun of sorts; only a few strands of my thick fringe edged around my face. She draped silver lacing on top of my hair and placed a sparkling blue gem on my forehead. She wrapped another around my small waist that trailed down to my tail. Eight small blue gems now shone amongst my black fur.

Siesta looked at me brightly with a smile, pulling away a piece of hair that was close to my eyes. "You look beautiful as always, my Princess. If only it were a full moon today, that would really bring out the shine of your eyes and gems."

I gave her a half smile. Ara barked at me, wagging her white tail. I patted my chest to permit her to jump up. I caught her before brushing over her fur. "Thank you, Siesta, for everything today."

I looked to the door, frowning in annoyance when I saw that Trim waited outside. I couldn't smell his scent over the steam in the air. I wasn't prepared for another confrontation. It seemed odd to me that I didn't sense him sooner. Since a young age our smell and instinctual awareness of each other had developed to the extent that we would always know where the other one was. We were so closely bonded that we were able to detect one another's presence the same way a mate might identify their partner. As I came closer to him my agitation lessoned. He was right and I spoke out in anger against him for no excusable reason.

He wore purple gems that trailed down his tail... *eight, the same number that I wear,* I noticed. The sparkling decorations drew my attention to his muscular legs, chiseled stomach, and broad chest. His arms were strong but not alarmingly huge. My gaze moved to the hard jaw that I always wanted to rest my hand on. His body was far too fit and attractive to ignore. I often thought that those wolves who had already confessed their feelings for him based their attraction not only on his appearance but on his strong, competent disposition. He epitomized both virtue and mystery in equal measures.

"I am sorry," I said quietly, unable to look into his eyes. Trim had been right for pulling me back from creating a scene, but instead of gratitude I had grown angry with him. Bathing had given me time to soothe my skin and calm my raging thoughts.

"You look beautiful tonight," Trim said contentedly. I looked up at him through wide eyes, surprised to hear him say such a thing. He held a small rose out and then looked away in discomfort. "I made you upset, and although only a flower, I thought—"

"It's perfect," I said, picking it out of his hand and spinning it in my fingers. Only moments ago I had been wishing for this very gift. I looked up at his face, which was now once again hard and unreadable. But it was there for one small moment. The Trim I had always wanted to know.

"Shall we now walk to the feast?"

I quickly caught up with his fast pace, still admiring the flower. No matter how hard his features, I had seen there was a considerate side to him. He had walked out into the gardens, thinking of me, and selected a rose. No matter how small a gesture, it was a large move on his behalf.

I looked at him with a small smile, unable to contain my happiness. I had had a terrible day, and yet with this one small gesture Trim had easily calmed me. To have him close was soothing. I boldly wrapped my hand around his arm and rested my head on it, which was warm against my ear. He flinched under my touch but did not shake me off like he usually would if I found a way to touch him. Whether he knew how I looked at him or not, I was grateful to have him so close and to have in my fingers the beautiful red rose he had given to me as a gift.

Chapter Seven- The Red and White Rose

The music was lively. Some wolves banged on hollow drums. One wolf placed an instrument to her mouth, placing her fingers over numerous holes and playing elegantly as she swayed with the music. Another plucked the long strings of another instrument encased in wood, playing it elegantly but with passion. Before we reached the stairs I stepped away from Trim. I couldn't show such affection for him in front of others. I had to keep my feelings for him a secret, unless he revealed a mutual affection. I couldn't bare others scrutinizing us or feeling pity for me because they were certain we were never to mate. Those words would only shatter my heart, so for now I kept him as close as one would any friend.

He waited for me to walk down the spiraled stairs before following me from behind. The music became louder as we approached. Many wolves danced jollily in the huge open space of the hall. On my left were my mother and father. They were seated side by side on decorated thrones, a magnificent table of food in front of them— a little too much food for my liking. Next to them was an empty chair, obviously kept for me. To my annoyance I noted that it was Fimble who was seated next to me.

Often Trim would sit by my side, but I guess on such an important night they would not cater for my preference of company. I greeted a few of the wolves that walked past as I made my way to my parents. I couldn't help but contain my smile as I was sure my father was now regretting the invitation he had extended to the loud, obnoxious pack. Their presence created a very different atmosphere to the one we usually enjoyed at banquets. Kratin laughed hysterically at something that obviously wasn't much to the amusement of my father. He then slapped him harshly on the back and my father's surprised reaction was that of a startled cub's.

Although my father wasn't overly big in build he handled a sword well. I often trained with him as a cub. My mother watched, she herself not much of a warrior. She wore a long chain of green gems that trailed past her chest to her stomach. She smiled gently at me. My eyes then met with Fiesca, who sat at the end with her brother, Lish. Her eyes deliberately trailed over Trim, enraging me. How I loathed her. She wore iridescent pink gems over her ears and a large matching gem right between her chest—drawing far too much attention to her bountiful assets, in my opinion.

"Sia, you finally came," Fimble said, quickly standing. Fimble wore silver gems that glided down the hair on his back to his tail. The jewelry complemented his gray fur as the gems caught the light of the flames that lit the room around us. There was an awkward tension when I reached to pull out my chair because as I did, both Trim's and Fimble's hands moved in unison to pull it back for me. They looked between one another suspiciously. I looked helplessly at my parents, who only gave me a wary look. Fimble sat down again in his seat, still watching Trim as he pulled my chair out for me. He stood strong behind me as I sat looking awkwardly at my parents. Fimble began to speak in a jovial tone, "Your presence is most gratefully received. I thought I would be waiting all evening."

"Apologies for my delay. There were a few errands I had to attend to," I said, placing a few slices of meat and chopped vegetables onto my plate. I looked back into my father's worried eyes; he looked as if he pitied me. I had not yet spoken to them since our argument. Although he had no intention of allowing me to entwine with a member of this pack, I was mortified to even hear him suggest it as a pretense. His blue eyes looked apologetic. I gave him a faint smile to let him know it was okay. For what reason he did it, I was not yet sure. But I had to trust him. I read no reproach in his eyes so I could only assume he was not aware of how the pack was initially greeted—by me edging an arrow into my suitor's throat.

"I was hoping that perhaps after you have eaten, we could share a dance and a walk together. I heard your gardens are beautiful and have many delightful flowers to see. I would very much appreciate it if you personally accompanied me," Fimble said forwardly.

I was holding my bowl to my lips, but upon his words I froze. I glanced sideways at my mother. He was so forward that I was taken aback. I placed the bowl down lightly and bent down to collect the red rose that was sitting beside my chair. "Of course," I agreed with a faint smile.

"Well, look at that, Lish, I don't think you have much of a chance in this," Kratin laughed, but the smile didn't reach his eyes. He did not actually find it funny and neither did I.

Lish barely noticed the comment. He was leering at some female wolves as if he wanted to ravish them. I would hate to think that any of my pack would want to entwine with such a repulsive wolf. And as for Fiesca, her eyes were still steady on Trim. She looked to be the middle sibling, perhaps the same age as Trim. Her brown eyes swept over him and then down to Ara, who sat with her nose raised at his feet, growling at her. I contained my smile. Ara obviously shared my dislike.

We all indulged in some light conversation, though my mother remained silent. She was watching over me cautiously. I had eaten my meal and was now fiddling with the red rose in my hand while Trim stood behind me in silence. I felt remorseful as he had not yet eaten and this was not how he was usually treated. We considered ourselves equals here at the palace and yet in the presence of Kratin's pack, we had created a hierarchy. Often when we had visitors at the castle Trim stood behind me like he did now, watching over me instead of eating with us. It unnerved me to never hear him complain, though usually the atmosphere was relaxed and cheerful. This pack obviously adhered to a system of judging people by their status and it created a strange atmosphere.

There was a sudden burst of loud chatter amongst the women. Hansel had made his entrance. They surrounded him and he somehow managed to flirt with all of them at once. I wondered at his charm. The women were instantly competitive, sure that they would be his chosen mate. He pardoned himself and came over to our table, where he offered his hand to Fiesca.

"My lady, may I have this dance?" he asked formerly with a sly smile. His expression made me ill. Somehow they seemed fitting for one another. She gave him an unimpressed look—as if even he were not worthy of her—before taking his hand and walking over with him to the dance floor. They perfectly suited each other physically, their height matching.

"Sia?" Fimble prompted, slightly nervous. His pale-brown eyes flickered with orange as his pupils reflected a nearby flame. "Shall we dance now?" He stood tall, pushing his chair aside so I could easily walk past. With hesitation I accepted his hand, which was surprisingly soft. I felt somehow guilty, but I was not abandoning my feelings for Trim. This was only a dance, but one I would have preferred to share with Trim. He walked me over to the center of the dance floor and I tried to ignore the wolves that watched and whispered. I peeled my ears back, unsure of what it was they said. I turned to Ara and Trim uncertainly, but Trim was already engrossed in conversation with my parents. My shoulders dropped—a small part of me thought that Trim might have minded. But he appeared as indifferent as always. Perhaps the red rose that still sat on the chair was only a friendly gesture.

Fimble gently set one of his hands on my hip while his other held my hand. His height was similar to my father's, who had taught me to dance. I gently rested my hands on his shoulders. There was not much difference from when I had practiced with my father. The music was light and slow as I watched the others who danced around us. Those who had already entwined were much closer to one another. They rested their heads against one another sweetly.

"I make you feel uncomfortable," Fimble said with disappointment. He was looking into my eyes evenly.

"No, no such thing," I said, embarrassed by my obvious discomfort. "I am sorry, I mean no disrespect. It is all just a little overwhelming for me right now."

"The talk of entwinement?" he asked forwardly. He swept me under his arm in a spin before gently pulling me back in.

"Partially, yes," I answered honestly. "I was only told of it yesterday. To be honest, I was surprised by it. I hadn't thought my parents would condone an arranged entwinement." I looked away, embarrassed at how easily I spoke the truth to Fimble. After he had spoken so easily it felt natural to do the same.

"It surprised my brother and I as well. But I wouldn't condemn you to the grief of my brother's company. You are too fine a wolf to deserve such a fate," he joked lightly. We both glanced over at the brutish wolf who tapped savagely at the table, obviously lusting after the female wolves. The ladies were too awed by Fiesca and Hansel to pay him much attention. Fimble spun me lightly under his arm, surprisingly very talented at dancing and taking the lead. I came back toward him and he held me closely from behind, his breath hot on my ear before flicking me back out and catching me in the gentle embrace we had started in.

"You can dance quite well," I said, impressed by his quick steps and easy, flowing movements.

"I know one would not expect it, especially considering how rudely my father and siblings act. For which, I do apologize," he added. "They are not the easiest to trust. But they do mean well." He seemed suddenly uneasy and I was unsure how to continue with the conversation. The music paused and he looked at me amiably before looking away with red across his cheeks.

"What is it?" I asked, intrigued by his sudden, shy smile.

"Would you like to show me to the gardens?" he enquired politely, his pale-brown eyes captivating me for a moment.

"Of course," I agreed, slowly slipping out of his hold. The music has stopped yet we had stayed in our embrace. As I turned, I was greeted by Trim's hard chest as I walked into him.

"Are you heading toward the gardens now, my lady?" Trim asked primly. He acted so different around others. His formality made me feel as though I were a stranger to him.

"Yes, we are, if you will pardon us..." Fimble said, offering his hand to me.

"Wonderful. I have been anxious to see the night sky tonight," Trim said with a slight hint of sarcasm. His stern face looked down intimidatingly on Fimble, as if daring him to reject his company. I said nothing as the two of them stared at one another in the thick atmosphere. I tentatively placed my hand on Fimble's arm, indicating that he may escort me to the gardens. He led me to the wooden doors of the castle entrance as Trim and Ara subtly followed.

Trim's words stuck in the back of my mind. He said for the next few days he would not leave my side. *Is this what he was anticipating, did he think me unsafe around this pack?* Fimble was so gently and mannerly I couldn't quite fathom the reason why Trim should shadow us. As I led Fimble to the gardens I looked up at the half-moon, which now shone brightly as the gray clouds parted. "Who was it that taught you how to dance?" I asked Fimble absentmindedly.

I looked back at Trim who watched me steadily, his face stern as always and his one blue eye looking back at me with scornfulness—a look I hadn't anticipated. Would it be cubbish of me to hope he was slightly jealous? But after all these years he could have made me aware if he had feelings. I dropped my head as I faced yet another hard reality. Trim did not love me, and I could not continue to delude myself with that fantasy.

"My mother; she was a very beautiful and gifted dancer," Fimble answered, also looking at the moon.

"Where is your mother now?"

"She was murdered by the hand of another pack's Alpha, they wanted our territory. Although they didn't win, they took something far greater. That was when I was aged nine. Since then, my father and elder siblings have focused on their fighting skills to protect our pack. They want to keep a savage reputation so no one else will try to take someone dear from us again. Often I think perhaps I am the only one who remembers her kind side. She would not have wanted us to fight or act wildly," he admitted as we walked into the magnificent gardens. Fimble looked to the sky as he told his story. As he finished he met my eyes and gave me a small smile.

"I am so sorry to hear of such an incident," I said earnestly. Ara rubbed against my ankle, making her presence known. I felt saddened at the thought of his suffering. I could not imagine losing my mother in such away, or at all. My parents were too dear to me to even contemplate them being torn away from me, especially by death.

"Such things happen, and cannot be taken back. We can only now look toward the future of our pack. Perhaps even you and I together," he said as he walked me over to one of the white rose bushes. He laughed lightly at my open mouth. "I will not pressure you into anything, Sia, but I want you to know you have made an impression on me. I hope that perhaps I have done the same." He snapped one of the white roses from the branch and offered it to me. The white rose was in elegant contrast to the shine of his gray hair and the lighter bronze of his skin. "This is what I wanted to come out to the gardens for."

"I don't know what to say," I exhaled, embarrassed.

"That is good," he laughed. "I had heard much of your beauty, but the rumors did not do you justice." He reached out and stroked my black hair.

"Fimble, forgive me if I seem rude, but you are very forward," I said, pulling away from him. "We have only just met." I looked at Trim nervously who still stood behind us, watching us. I felt embarrassed to have had such a conversation in front of Trim—even if his face was expressionless.

"Sorry, I have been told before that I am too forward with my intentions and words. But it surprised me, when you attacked me at first. I expected a fragile, beautiful creature; someone vain and shallow. After all you are young, and a Royal at that. And yet when you attacked me when we first met, I was surprised by your bravery and your passion. You mirrored me in a way. You did not try to hide your abruptness or your beliefs. That is the true beauty I saw in you. Your words may have been savage, but when you held that arrow to my throat I knew you wouldn't do such a thing. Although you were in pain because we hunted the young doe, your heart is too pure for you to become a killer. That is the beauty I see in you."

The wind rustled through my thick black hair. My mind raced over so many things. No one had ever described me in such a way. No one had ever claimed to see my true beauty. I had never met someone like Fimble. Slowly I took the white rose, noticing the small orange insect it contained. This rose was not perfect, much like myself.

"I am sorry to be so forward and to put these thoughts out so openly, but I cannot apologize for how I feel about you. I have no reason to lie to you. The truth is, I would like to spend more time with you and learn more about you... how your pack differs from my own. I don't expect that you will immediately agree, but I would appreciate if you thought on it tonight, Sia."

"Sia," Trim interrupted as he stepped forward, taking my breath away. I was too stunned for words. "Your father is calling for you. Perhaps it is too cold of a night to be out any longer."

I looked from his blue beautiful eye to Fimble's pale-brown ones. "Perhaps," I said, wondering what my father would think of Fimble's declared intentions. I turned from Fimble with no other words passing my lips. I walked toward the castle, almost striding to get away from the confession. I was unsure what to do in such a situation. Ara followed me, as did Trim, who quickly put distance between Fimble and me. Fimble had somehow managed to crawl beneath my skin. I could not understand why and hated that I was so unbalanced by his words.

"Where is my father?" I asked Trim quickly, now embarrassed that I had practically run away.

"He did not call," Trim said. He returned my quizzical stare with an even look. "I saw you were uncomfortable so I made the decision for you. You should retreat to your room. I imagined it would have only been another few minutes before you ran, at least this way I did not have to chase you."

I looked at him in disbelief, surprised that he had created such a cunning lie. And yet I could not be infuriated by him, because he was very right. I needed time to compose myself and decipher these thoughts. I could not just dismiss Fimble's words, as I did with Hansel. He was genuine, and I could not handle how my heart raced and my mind scattered with his words. But in Trim's presence I felt calm and protected by only looking at him. How could my body possibly react in such a way to two completely different wolves? One I had known and cherished my whole life, and the other I had only just met.

Chapter Eight- Eerie Thoughts

In the darkness of the night I had the sudden urge to visit Lady Momiko, as if she were calling for me. I couldn't shake the feeling off as I constantly awoke to her whispering my name. Eventually I was too consumed by panic to sleep and I quietly sneaked out of my room. I walked up the spiral staircase holding a stick with a flame on top that lit my path. For some reason Ara was not with me. The castle was silent as the cool chill of night air swept through its walls.

An eeriness swept over me as I reached where the hallway forked. On my right was Lady Momiko's resting room and on my left were the bathing chambers. Something light dropped to the ground in the bathing chambers, grabbing my attention as it bounced off the floor.

"Hello?" I called, questioning who would be walking around at such a late hour. Following the noise, I took steps toward the bathing chambers in suspicion. The flash of a shadow caught my eye beside me and I quickly swung the flame to light up the area.

"Is somewhere there?" I called out. I wondered if this was a trick of some kind. For so long my parents had joked, "have you ever heard that curiosity killed the wolf?" I wondered if perhaps this was their way of trying to scare me into being good.

The shadow streaked behind me again and I swung the flame just as quickly, startled that they could move so fast. "This really isn't funny," I stated, now annoyed by such cubbish games. I remembered the true intention of this investigation and I began walking down the hall to Lady Momiko's room. I instinctively quickened my pace as I felt someone follow me, and to my surprise my heart pattered. I found I was now fearful that it was someone unfamiliar who followed.

A shadow streaked in front of me with a low whistling noise that was comparable to when wind brushes past your ears. I stretched the flame high, still not noticing anyone. Lady Momiko's door was only steps away. I hurried toward it and opened the door, still seeing no one. I closed the door behind me, closing my eyes briefly in relief.

Holding myself tightly I opened my eyes. I screamed at the sight I then saw before me, dropping my flame onto the cement floor. I cried as I cupped my hands over my mouth, trying to contain my horrified scream.

Lady Momiko's sheets were bloodied. Her hand hung over her bed and blood dripped down her arm. Her mouth was still open as if she had screamed and no one had heard. Or had I heard and not come in time? Her eyes looked directly ahead of her as if she stared at the killer, who had obviously stabbed her numerous times.

Banging noises began, it sounded as if someone was hitting near her wooden bed. A breeze swept through the window, tearing down the fur pelts that blocked the moon and wind. They flew at my face and covered my eyes. I screamed in horror, unable to run to Lady Momiko as my legs trembled. The breeze blew out the flames that crackled at my feet. My screams ceased and I listened—I heard the footsteps coming closer. I was shaking so severely that I could not run or hide; I simply stood, my face in my hands. I felt hot breath on my neck but I was unable to look up at he who was about to kill me. I could not move or scream. I was utterly defenseless.

*

I gasped in horror, smacking away attacking hands and punching into the dark shadow that had bent over me as I slept.

"Sia! Sia, it is me!" A familiar voice pleaded. His hands were on my shoulders, gently shaking me. I paused for a moment, my eyesight now focusing clearly on Trim's familiar frame.

"Trim?" I said shakily, trying to awake from my delirium. *It was just a dream.*

"It's me," he whispered again, pulling me closer and holding me. I clutched desperately onto him, my arms wrapping around his back. I sobbed into his neck. "It was just a dream," he soothed, stroking over the back of my hair. I breathed heavily, trying to regain my breath.

"Lady Momiko... and I, there was blood... and..." I gasped. I could not force out the words as panic descended over me yet again. I recalled the vivid image of her death with each word that I stuttered.

"Lady Momiko is okay." He cupped my face hard, his blue eye staring at me intently. I avoided his gaze and he shook me lightly so that I focused on him. He spoke quietly to me, calming me as I inhaled his words, "It was just a dream. Everything is okay. You're all right."

I accepted his words. I shook my head as I noticed that I was hot and sticky from sweat. He slowly let me go and I regained my breath, absorbed the night air from my window. The half-moon still shone through my windows although it was almost completely covered with gray clouds.

Ara placed her white paw on my arm in concern, whimpering as her big blue eyes looked up at me. Trim sat on the edge of my bed with me. I focused on my room, forcing myself to become aware of my familiar surroundings. "Thank you," I whispered gently, frowning in disbelief that a nightmare had traumatized me so badly. I had never had such a dream. "Lady

Momiko?" I asked, the memory of her still raw. I knew it was just a dream but still had to check that she really was all right.

"She is okay." His expression slightly changed, and he frowned. "What happened in your dream?"

I was surprised that he was curious about what I had seen. I swallowed the lump that was in my throat, recalling the scene. "There was a wolf, and he stalked me. I walked into Lady Momiko's room, scared... and when I turned..." I paused, her open mouth and dripping arm vividly coming to my mind. "He had killed her."

A silence swept over us. Now that I was calm I suddenly felt very aware that it was only Trim and me in my room. I flushed red at the thought—my body was already hot. I was still and silent, unable to manage my thoughts. My hand still lingered on his arm and my fingers rested on his stiff hair. I noticed the difference between the size of his arms and my own. His build was so large that I was desperate for him to cocoon me in warmth. I stared at his lips. They parted, as if he were going to speak. But he said nothing, his face as unreadable as always. I lightly trailed my hand over his arm, unsure of why my hand wanted so badly to linger on his hot skin.

He looked at my lingering hand and tightened his jaw. He dipped his head to hide his expression from me as he contemplated my touch. My fingers reached his open hand; his skin was so coarse compared to the softness of my own. His fingers twitched under my touch as I looked up at him. I was curious to know if he wanted to touch my skin as much as I did his.

I leaned toward him. My forehead was so close to his and his lips were so reachable and yet untouchable. I hesitated, wanting his hot breath on mine. I could feel his heat rising as my own did, and his tail started to flicker back and forth. I looked up again, hoping to see a reflection of my own desire in his eyes. If his body reacted this way with me so close to him, then surely it meant he wanted the same thing. I leaned in toward him, brushing my nose against his and looking for consent to kiss him. He stiffened under my touch. He moved slightly toward me then paused before pulling away with a heavy breath.

I sat there stunned, embarrassed for getting so carried away. I let a cool breath out, feeling as though I hadn't been breathing properly because of how intensely I desired him.

"If you need me, I will be outside," he said, moving to leave.

In a second he had crossed the room. I called out to him. "Trim?" I asked, grabbing his attention before he closed the door. Hesitantly he looked at me, his blue eye shimmering in the glow of the moon. It was as though he was scared of what I might ask. "Why are you watching over me so much lately?"

Trim stared back at me, as if weighing his words. His expression was considerate rather than scornful. "It is my job. These are precious days to come. Your parents asked me to guard you."

I thought about this, still suspicious of his motives. No one would tell me the secrets they hid from me. I could only be grateful that he was there, without him there would have been no one to calm me after such a horrific dream.

"Thank you," I quickly said, before he closed the door completely, leaving me and Ara to ourselves. I placed my hand on my forehead, surprised by how much I had sweated. I was embarrassed for what I had just done so I closed my eyes to try and forget. *I will never think of this embarrassing moment again.* I patted my face now as it cooled. My thoughts drifted between Trim's hard arms that had embraced me and the memory of when he had grabbed my face to snap me out of my fear-stricken state.

Looking at the closed door, I began chewing the nail of my thumb in thought. Although he said it was nothing and only a dream, I couldn't shake the realistic imagery from my mind. I crouched down to the floor, picking up the fur pelts I had flicked off in my restless sleep. A dim blue glow caught my attention. I reached my hand under my wooden bed, pulling out the ragged stone. Lady Momiko's gift. I felt as though I were hypnotized as I stared at it. I couldn't help but feel that there was something more to the dream than Trim would admit.

I closed my fist around it as my mind raced. *Is something happening that no one is willing to tell me?* The last few days my parents had been acting oddly and now Trim was as well. I sat on my bed, unable to sleep as I stared at the moon. Shortly after rain began to pour. Still I stayed awake. I patted Ara back to sleep while I tried to find a connection between my dream and the mysterious moonstone.

Chapter Nine- Living Creatures

$\mathscr{S}$omewhere amongst all my thoughts—even though I had promised myself I wouldn't torture myself about how I had thrown myself on Trim—I fell asleep still sitting upright against the wall, moonstone in hand. When I slowly opened my eyes and wiped away the sleep, I noticed the moonstone was no longer glowing, as if it had all been my imagination.

"Good Morning, Princess Sia," Siesta called from across the room. She picked a few of the fur pelts off the floor from when I had flicked them off during my sleep. She looked at them in confusion as she collected them, then walked over to my bed and patted Ara in greeting.

"Good Morning Siesta," I said yawning and stretching. My back ached from my awkward sleep.

"You should get ready quickly, breakfast will be served soon," she encouraged, pulling out the wooden chair from near my desk and offering it out to me. Groggily I walked over to it. I couldn't help but look to the closed door and wonder if Trim was still there watching over me. Siesta tugged at my hair as she braided my thick black fringe and pinned it behind loosely so it would not be in my eyes for the day. She brushed through my hair and my tail before giving me an approving look, obviously pleased with her work.

I looked back toward the sun that had only just risen, surprised that Siesta had come so early. Breakfast was not usually served until later.

"Siesta, why are we getting ready so early?" I asked, now fully awake.

"That is my fault," Trim said sternly, opening my door.

I held myself with dignity, trying to not let red creep across my cheeks. I didn't want Siesta to pick up on what had happened. *It's behind me; never will I think of such embarrassment again*, I promised myself.

"It is your eighteenth birthday tomorrow. So I thought, for once, I should permit you to leave the castle walls... upon the condition that I escort you, of course."

"Do my parents know of this?" I asked curiously, narrowing my eyes on him in suspicion. Despite how much I begged him, this was a wish he very rarely granted.

"Sia, do you think we would be leaving so early if they did?" he asked. I smiled in return, genuinely happy. Siesta left the room and I jumped off my chair, excited that we could go for a walk. At least this time I wouldn't be chased.

"I have a gift for you," he said quietly, not able to look me in the eyes as he held his hand out to me. A thick piece of silver shone out and he motioned for me to turn around. I did so and his rough fingers trailed over my skin as he lifted my hair clumsily. I helped him, lifting my heavy hair for him as his arms wrapped around my neck. My heart raced as I felt his warmth so close to my back. A light coolness pressed against my chest. I took hold of the material and lifted it to examine it better. One large blue moonstone was the centerpiece of the jeweled string, and another four trailed up the thick silver, two on either side. I dropped my hair as he took a step back, looking at me in admiration. *Why has he given me this?*

"I hope the celebrations of your eighteenth are memorable, Sia. Lady Momiko suggested that you might like such a gift," he carefully said with an unreadable expression. I smiled at the present; it was certainly not expected. I couldn't help but notice he had selected moonstones. After what had happened last night, and the gifts that Lady Momiko had given me, the coincidence unsettled me.

"It is not yet my day," I said, teasing him. Something seemed odd about him, his expression was more open. Trim was revealing a much softer side to me.

"The way you act on most, you would think every day is your day," he said rudely before walking toward the door. "Shall we go for a walk now before everyone else has wakened?"

I slipped past him, excited that he had finally given me permission to leave. I looked forward to running with the deer and watching the tranquil water flow down the waterfall I admired so much. Hopefully the bear would be there today hunting for fish once again. I always enjoyed watching nature at its most primal moments.

I hurriedly walked through the huts toward the large opening in front of me. Only a few wolves were up at this time and they greeted us warmly as we walked past. I sniffed, smiling at the new scent. Siesta had recently informed me that Robyn was due to give birth to her second cub. The new male scent told us that last night he had arrived safely. I smiled brightly but Trim looked unfazed by the same scent. Perhaps it was because he was a male that he didn't celebrate that a new little cub had joined our pack.

Ara pranced beside me, keeping at my pace. As soon as I walked through the castle walls I ran freely, thrilled to have the sun glimmering in my eyes. I ran for the trees, listening to the sounds of the animals. The animals scattered and I trained my ears on the sound of galloping hooves. Trim chased me as I ran faster, trying to outrun him, but as usual he was too fast for me and he ran ahead, challenging me. Like always, I could not refuse.

Finally the pounding of my heart synced with the pounding of the hooves. My ears pulled back—I had found them. Trim followed me but stopped at the trees. He watched me from afar as I called out to them. They parted for me and I began running, smiling happily at Ara by my side. I hid amongst them, challenging them all in speed and panting heavily with exhilaration at such a glorious morning run.

I ran from the shade of the trees into an open green field. I began to slow, my legs hot from the run. My ears pulled back as I inhaled the freshly stomped grass. The birds' songs soothed me into a serene state of mind. This was my life, and here amongst all the animals, it was peaceful. I inhaled the fresh air once again, finding an unfamiliar smell amongst it. I sniffed again, uncertain of this new smell. It was neither from an animal nor a wolf that I could recognize. I let the deer run past me so their nearby smell wouldn't taint my own. I looked back at Trim, who stood far from me, looking in my direction. He appeared to have registered the same smell I did.

There was a scent, one from an animal I had never smelled before, and with it there was blood. Instinctively I ran toward it; perhaps our visitors had once again hunted on our land. Trim yelled out my name, but he was too far away from me to be able to hold me back.

I ran into the trees, swiping away the branches that grazed my face. Green blurred around me from the leaves of the trees and bushes as I focused only on the unknown scent. I could no longer hear the singing of the birds as I focused my hearing on the heavy panting of this unfamiliar creature. I found the shadow of a wolf that ran much slower than me. I jumped on him, throwing him to the ground. We rolled together on the ground and we came to a stop with me on top of him. I pinned my knee to his throat as I took in his unique brown eyes. He coughed into my chest as I held my hand high above his body, ready to use my nails as a weapon if I had to.

As he struggled to breathe I looked over his face. My eyes widened as I realized he was not a wolf at all. He did not have wolf ears or a tail—only thin, mousy-brown hair and tanned skin. His frame was bulkier then mine and yet my strength overpowered his instantly.

I jumped off the foreign creature. Crouching low to the ground, I watched him with interest. He wrapped his hand around his throat, coughing. I realized there was another smell. It was very light, not a distinctive one. It was not a smell I would associate with any of my pack or any other wolves.

I turned my head in the direction of the scent. There stood a cub of sorts. She looked like a cub, yet she did not have wolf ears or a tail. She had long honeycomb hair which came to her lower back and brown eyes—like the male. At a guess, she was between six and seven, while the male was around my age. Their combined scents suggested they were siblings.

The male scampered over to his sister. Clutching her protectively, he continued to watch me cautiously in silence. The girl began to sob as Ara slowly walked over to her.

"Ara!" I growled. My little white friend did not heed my warning; instead she walked over to her so she could smell her hand. The male watched her guardedly. He moved to pull back the young girl as she slowly reached her hand out for Ara to sniff it.

"What are you?" I asked curiously, my head leaning to the side as I watched Ara walk around him. If Ara was brave enough to walk toward the little one, then that was enough of an indicator that they were harmless. They wore an odd, thin material which covered the entirety of their bodies. I noticed the smell of blood again and I looked at the girl's bleeding shin. It bled quickly but the blood was much thinner than that of my own kind.

I sensed Trim and seconds later he broke out of the trees. He paused as he took in the scene before him. His chest rose and fell quickly and his eye narrowed on the male. The girl was instantly frightened and screamed in fear of him. Trim growled horrifically. Never had I seen such hatred in his eye. When he ran for the child I instinctively threw myself on him, pulling him to the ground. I pinned him down. Thankfully, because I had caught him off guard, I had momentary control of him. The look he shot me paralyzed me with dread. No words needed to be exchanged as a tear shed from his eye from rage. His face was contorted and red—it seemed as though he barely seen me. The look in his eye was not a familiar sight.

I thought of all the stories told about human existence. They were humans, those creatures with the infamous power to turn us into Phantom Wolves. Many dismissed their kind as a mere myth, but I knew better. My parents, Trim, and Lady Momiko all spoke of one terrible being who had ruined Sia's life with such a curse.

The little girl's screaming pierced my ears and pained my chest. Although I sympathized with his reasoning, I could not allow him to murder such a young creature. I understood his pain; I knew of my parents' warnings. And yet, my chest pained for her— such innocence could not contain evil. I depended on Ara's judgment of other wolves often, and in this case, she had gone to them willingly, believing them to be harmless.

Trim threw me off. I skidded along the earth, my feet and hands grabbing at the soil. Already the humans had begun to flee. I jumped back toward him, not giving him the chance to pursue them. I kicked Trim in the stomach to stop him from running toward them. He blocked it, elbowing me in the back of the leg. I dropped and held my breath at the pain. I clung to his leg when he tried to run again. When I looked up I saw that he had raised his hand, preparing to use force to hit me away.

I opened my eyes wide and tilted my head to look up at him. He stopped himself from committing the violent action just in time. Tears dropped onto my face as for the first time he cried in front of me. They were tears of rage that could not be contained. My mouth widened as I did not know what to say to him. It was a human who had killed his mentor, Sia. His rage had been tormenting him for years.

Will he hate me now because I pulled him back from justice?

"She is only a cub," I whispered, using it as an excuse to draw him away from his murderous rage. Never had I seen his composure so shattered. Never had he raised a hand to me. His actions were inexcusable—not because I was royalty, but because I was his friend. I did not think it was me he saw when he raised his fist. That was not in Trim's nature.

"They are murderers," he hissed. These were not his words; he was repeating a label he had been taught as he grew up. I had to make him see the humans now as we found them: alone, scared, vulnerable, *harmless*. His body shook as I stood up and pulled him toward me. I held him tightly, trying to provide him with the same comfort with which he had always afforded me. We looked together into the direction that the humans had fled. *Did Trim only stop because I asked him? Was my request more important to him than his need for revenge?*

Slowly his body stopped trembling as I stroked through his orange hair, consoling him tenderly. I did not know what to do in such a situation. Never had he broken in front of me like this, revealing such a sensitive side. I thought again of the cub he must have been, watching in horror as my uncle Kiba and his lover were torn apart over the curse. He so bravely went up against another wolf to help them—a courageous act that scarred him for life.

This pivotal part of his life had left him damaged and introverted. He had contained his rage and his despair, unable or unwilling to reveal it to anyone. Lady Momiko's words echoed through my mind. She had told me to look after him. Is this what she had meant?

Ara walked over to us slowly, still looking into the direction the humans had run into. Although their scent was faint, they could be easily traced and captured. We did not give chase.

Trim's hand rested on my back and suddenly he seemed very aware of our contact. He grabbed my hip and pushed me away, his hand no longer using me for support. His jaw clenched as he turned his head, hiding his eye from me. All I could see was the scarring on his face.

"Why would you let them go?" he said angrily, making me wince under his harsh stare. If it was anyone else I would have stood against them. My words would have been like acid in their face. And yet when Trim spoke to me in such a tone I only wanted to retreat and crumble into myself.

"No matter what creatures they were, they meant no harm," I said soothingly, trying to make him see reason. We could not kill them because we feared them. It was not our Kingdom's way of dealing with predators on our land, so why make an exception for them? Although the stories spoke of monsters that relished our kind's extinction, when I looked into both the cub and the male's brown eyes, I could not see murderers within.

"You don't know that, Sia. You just don't!" He pulled away from me and shrugged off my outstretched arm. "I am informing your parents about this at once. You have endangered every wolf they encounter."

"Please don't!" I begged, curling my hands to my chest. My fingers fidgeted with the moonstones on my chest. I did not even know why I was trying to protect the humans or keep them a secret. "I don't want to watch a hunt."

"They are humans!" he yelled, throwing his hand in their direction.

"They are alive. They have a heart, a pulse... they are living creatures!" I yelled back, my voice shaky. "I will not forgive you if

88

you kill them just because you are grieving for your past!" I stood by my words, but Trim looked as though I had slapped him in the face.

Why am I protecting these humans? Instinctively I wanted to protect all that was living. But these living creatures were not murderers. They were lost and frightened. It pained me to face my beliefs at the cost of standing against Trim. Perhaps I should be standing with Trim instead of against him, but somehow I just couldn't.

Unable to look away from one another, our chests rose and fell from our outburst. "You don't know anything of my past," he whispered. His words felt as if they pulled my heart out, taking my breath away. "We are going back."

He was right. I did not know of his past, he had never told me. All I knew were the stories I had heard from Lady Momiko and my parents. He became more guarded as we grew together. I knew of his parents. His father was murdered by another pack just after his birth. Although their village was victorious in keeping their territory, Lady Momiko said many died. His father—one of their finest warriors—was murdered for this cause. Shortly after, his mother died of a sudden illness and Lady Momiko took him in. What little I knew I did not learn from him. He was unwilling to share with me. I felt as though everyone I loved conspired to keep me in the dark.

Ara led me past Trim and I avoided eye contact with him. I was not ashamed for what I said, only saddened by the pain it caused us both. He followed me to the castle under the bright morning sun.

How do I force him to keep this a secret? I wondered. *I do not want a hunt to begin.* There was a tightening in my chest that restricted my breath when I thought of the humans. For some reason, whether it was instinct or something else, I had to keep those humans alive.

Chapter Ten- Conspiracy

Trim followed me from a distance as I walked through the castle's walls. We did not speak as we had travelled back and I knew we probably wouldn't for many days now. The back of my leg no longer hurt. He had only struck me hard enough to drop me to the ground. I couldn't blame him for that; it was I who had struck him first—he was defending himself against me.

My memory focused on the faces of the male and the child. The humans I had seen for the first time. They looked so similar to us and yet they were completely different. They seemed so fragile, so easily broken. And to think it was these delicate creatures that my kind had feared for so long. When I held the human male I was significantly more powerful than him. I overthrew him quite easily. I could have killed him instantly. So how had their kind now killed three of ours? How did they gain such advantage when we were so obviously superior in strength?

"Princess Sia!" Siesta yelled out at me, frantically running toward me.

"What is it Siesta? What has happened?" I asked, trying to keep my voice low so others would not hear our conversation. The ears of other wolves pricked up in curiosity.

She caught her breath before lowering her tone and speaking to me in a hushed, panicked tone. "It is Lady Momiko. She has gone; no one knows where she has hidden."

Instinctively I looked into the direction of her window, the wild imagery of my previous night's dream flashing before my eyes. I looked back at Trim in concern and saw that he had overheard our conversation. He too was staring at her window, his orange ears pinned back, yet his face was an expressionless mask.

"Is anyone looking for her?" I asked Siesta, fiddling anxiously with the large moonstone between my breasts.

"Yes, some of the guards. Hansel himself is leading the search. They suspect she left of her own free will as there is no sign of a struggle or a break-in. We have questioned the people who have been caring for her but there has been no suspicious activity noted."

"Do my parents know of this?" I asked. My mind was already on the real question at hand. Why would Lady Momiko leave when she was on death's door already?

"Yes, your mother is currently waiting in the library for you until the guests assemble for breakfast. I told her I was waking you so you could quickly go to her," Siesta confirmed.

"Trim, will you go in search of Lady Momiko?" It was not a question, more of an order. I wanted Lady Momiko safe and resting.

"I cannot leave your side."

I did not stop to argue with him. I quickened my pace. I felt as though he knew something I didn't. *Does he know where Lady Momiko has ventured to? What is everyone keeping from me?*

As I reached the stairs, Fimble announced himself from the Great Hall in which we had feasted last night. "Good morning, Sia. Why are you in such a rush?"

"I am sorry, Fimble, but I cannot talk right now," I said, running up the stairs. His gray ears flattened and his brown eyes dropped to the ground. I felt rude for my sudden abruptness but I was frantic about Lady Momiko and eager to hear what my mother had to say.

I pulled open the wooden doors of the library and the flickering flames of the fire instantly caught my eye. My mother was staring into the fire despondently. Startled by my sudden entrance, she rose and held her hands out to me.

"I do not know where she has gone, my Sia," my mother said as I rushed into her arms and hugged her.

"Are we investigating her disappearance? Has someone taken her?" I interrogated. Thoughts washed over me as I felt panic rise in my throat. It seemed the images of my nightmare had come to fruition. I desperately hoped she had not been hurt. Perhaps she had fled from her attacker. It would haunt us all forever if she had endured any pain or fear before her death. I wanted to at least say goodbye properly.

"It looks as if she has gone of her own accord," my mother said, stroking my black fringe.

"Then we must search for her, she is already not well. She will only survive her illness if she is cared for. Trim? You must go in search of her," I commanded over my shoulder.

"I cannot leave you," he answered from behind me. I saw that he was looking past me to my mother. I looked between them and witnessed my mother's tight lips and pale skin.

"You know something, and yet you will not tell me," I accused, both hurt and angry.

My mother cupped my face as she began to speak soothing lies. "Sia, my sweet—"

I stepped back, giving her a hurt glare. "I am so sick of never being good enough, of never being deemed as an equal or treated like the woman I am," I said, my words trembling. "You cannot continuously keep controlling my life."

I turned my attention to Trim. "I am sick of you relentlessly following me without telling me why. I am no one's pet, and will not be treated as such." I stormed past him, holding in tears.

Constantly I was shadowed, watched over. I felt like I could never breathe. My instinct that something was wrong was mounting, yet no one trusted me with the information that would placate my tortured mind. How was that protecting me?

My pace quickened as I went down the stairs, deeply inhaling as I felt like I could not properly breathe. My body was tense and hot as I trembled in anger.

"Oh no, did the Princess get sent to her room?" Fiesca taunted.

Her words struck like a snake biting into my chest. My fists trembled by my side as I forced myself to walk calmly down the stairs. I tried to avoid her but she walked deliberately into my path.

"I am talking to you," she savagely spat, grabbing my wrist.

A burst of anger rushed through me that I could not control. I backhanded her hand from mine, releasing her hold of me. She jumped back with a smile. It was a smile of challenge. Finally she had gotten what she wanted.

She came at me, her palm aiming for my face. I dodged it, aiming to knee her in the stomach, but she blocked me. She thrust her elbow into my face but I ducked, kicking at her shins. She quickly jumped back to avoid my hit.

Her claws grazed by my chest as I jumped back against the staircase. I wrapped my arms around the small bars so they could support my weight and then I lifted myself and kicked at her face as she charged at me. She grabbed my legs, throwing me from the firm grip I had of the railing. She threw me down the last few stairs so I was now lying on the cement floor beneath the staircase. I winced on the ground at the sudden impact, but managed to roll to the side before her leg came down over my face.

I blocked her two fists, still lying on my back. Before she could hit out again, I rested my weight on my right elbow as I swung my left leg across to her face. I knocked her away from me before crouching and then standing. I ran for her, leaping onto her back as she fumbled to stand again. I wrapped my legs around her waist, grabbing her arms and pinning them back.

Fimble suddenly burst out from the Great Hall, his eyes large as he watched us. Fiesca slammed me into the wall, crushing me before I fell off her. She smashed her knee into my forearms as I held them up for protection. Her quick hands grabbed my black hair, pulling me into a standing position. I looked into her large eyes with anger. She raised her claws to me, ready to plunge them into my throat. Ara's white fur suddenly flickered at the side of my eye. She latched onto Fiesca's arm, pulling it back and forth. Ara hung off her, snarling. Fiesca dropped me, ripping at the back of Ara's neck and flinging her across the room.

"Ara!" I screamed. I growled at Fiesca, burrowing my head deep into her stomach as I tackled her to the ground, punching into her. Quickly she was on top of me, her weight far greater than my own. As it took her several hits to try and break the block I created in front of my face with my arms, she punched into my chest, taking away my breath.

I was too winded to hold my arms up any longer and they dropped to the sides. She took aim for my face, but before she could plunge her clenched fist into me she was ripped off my body and flung against the wall. Trim's orange tail flickered vigorously as he hunched over me, his claws scratching into the floor. Deep snarls ripped from his throat as he blanketed me in protectiveness.

Fimble stood in front of his sister with his hands in front of her. She gathered herself, ready to pounce on Trim.

"That is enough, Fiesca!" Fimble's voice hardened into a tone so rough it felt as though it tore strips off my skin. Authority emanated from him—his eyes, his stance, his tone. Fiesca's ears pinned back as she looked at her brother. She patted herself gently before walking away into the direction that she had come, her hips swaying from side to side as she looked back at me. Her look suggested that I was to understand our feud was not over.

I gasped for my lost breath as Ara scampered over. She seemed unscathed. I curled myself around her, sobbing that I had let such a thing happen to her. *How could I have let her be hurt by that wolf? Why was I unable to protect her?* But I was so sure I could protect myself no matter what.

Trim's hand lightly touched my back. I hid my face in Ara's fur as I sobbed. I held her closely as I raised myself from the ground.

"Sia, I am so sorry," Fimble's voice rang out with sincerity. I hesitated to look at him.

"Your declaration of admiration was truly proved. You did nothing until you were forced to protect your sister," Trim said harshly as his hand gently pressed on my back again, pushing me toward my room. I was hurt by Trim's words because they were true. Fimble hadn't intervened. But how could I expect him to stand against his sister? And yet, a small part of me thought he would protect me.

"It wasn't like that!" Fimble yelled from behind us. As I reached the darker side of the hall his words carried to me in a small whisper, "Sia, I am so sorry."

Chapter Eleven- Unspoken Words

"*We* must put something cool on your shoulder, its bruising," Trim said as he led me into my room. I opened my door and the first object to catch my eye was Lady Momiko's stick that she had gifted me. Still I did not understand why she had given it to me; it was of no use to me. I wondered if Trim would comment on it but he seemed fixated on my injuries.

I rolled my shoulder slightly, wincing. Trim had predicted it would bruise, he was right. "It will be fine," I said distantly. It was because I was too weak to protect myself that I was injured. My pride was not something that could be so quickly healed.

"She grabbed me first," I explained, already preparing to defend my case. I knew he would lecture me, and I knew my parents would frown upon my actions and be displeased. But I could not bottle such anger in and have such a wolf openly mock me. What stung me most was that she was right about the protective state everyone blanketed me in. She had mirrored my very thoughts. I was told what to do and I was expected to do it. It was as if I was fighting my own thoughts through fighting her. I looked over my shoulder at Trim calculatingly. They hid something from me even though they all knew I had my suspicions.

"I know she did," he said considerately. His blue eye looked back at me evenly, and then to my shoulder. *My injured shoulder should be of no consequent to him, unless of course he wants to discuss his effectiveness in "guarding" me*, I thought unkindly. I pulled my long black hair to the side, covering my shoulder so he could no longer see.

My ears pinned back as I detected the sound of clashing weapons. I walked over to my open window and looked down over the hedges where I often trained. There fought Lish and Hansel, clashing swords as they smiled viciously at one another. They seemed to be relishing the chance to test their skills against another pack.

Trim brushed past me to look over my shoulder. His chin was so close to the top of my head. He watched them as I did. They were both equally matched.

"Why are they really here?" I asked. Trim's presence no longer hovered over me as he walked back toward the door.

"Your father wishes to make an allegiance with them. It is instrumental that we befriend this pack," he answered. He spoke as if I hadn't heard it all before. I had. He only repeated the same lies, always cautious with the big secret.

"And if I were to be palmed off, to have to entwine with one of the brothers…" I began in a carefree tone. I glanced at him for a split-second to register the effect of my words before continuing. I knew I had piqued his interest as his ears had perked up. "…Would you find that advantageous for the goal that you and my father share?"

The atmosphere was heavy as he said nothing. His silence only confirmed his disinterest in me. I bit down on my lip, slightly shaking my head at my foolishness. *He does not care. If anything, if I were to entwine with another he would no longer have to guard me… he would probably be free.*

"Lady Sia," Siesta interrupted as she pushed past Trim, looking between us oddly. "My goodness, what have you done to your hair in such a short space of time?" She rushed over to me in a fluster before pulling the stool out for me to sit down on so she could tidy my hair. She gave Trim a suspicious look, which made him streak red across his cheeks. He walked out, with his composure still intact.

I was surprised she had not yet heard of my confrontation with Fiesca. I was immensely grateful that no other wolves were around to witness what had happened. The news would spread very quickly of my defeat.

"Siesta, what is it you do in your spare time when you are not catering for my needs?" I asked curiously, wondering what it would be like to be living as another wolf.

"That is an unexpected question, my lady," she frowned as she looked up. "I often like to pick fruit; apples are my father's favorite. I often go out into the orchard to pick them. I also like to dance; I and a few likeminded wolves dance together every full moon. Although we must go out to the gardens where no one can hear or see us. Two of my companions can play the musical instruments, although not as well as those who play at royal events."

"Is there any wolf you have your eyes on for entwinement? Or perhaps you already know the amount of cubs you wish to have?" I asked boldly. She stopped pulling my hair for a moment as she looked at me. After much contemplation she answered.

"There is a wolf I admire from afar, but I think he is out of my league. I often even think that perhaps he has eyes for another. She is a respectable wolf whom I wouldn't want to stand against. If it is not my love then it will not reach out for me," she hesitated for a moment before adopting a more upbeat attitude. "But I wish to have as many cubs as possible someday. I am an only cub and wish for my family to be vast, I couldn't wish for anything better than nurturing my own young cubs so that they become fine wolves."

I smiled at her. Siesta's optimistic attitude put me instantly at ease. Siesta often made me calm as she looked after me, so I could imagine she would be a wonderful mother, much like my own.

I softly patted Ara as she sat on my lap contentedly, also listening to Siesta talk. Another wolf came to the door of my room. I had seen her around the castle but didn't associate with her often; she seemed timid around me and cautious with her words. I wondered if wolves would be looser with their tongue if they knew the real me. "May I speak, Princess Sia?" The red-haired wolf asked, curtsying. Upon my nod she continued. "A few of our guards are conversing with the unfamiliar pack. They are making a display of their skills. Fimble, the one who has taken a liking to you, my lady..." Her eyes dropped to the ground as I gave her a discouraging look. " I am sorry to speak out of context. I am here upon his request that I plead for your attendance... Fimble has requested that you come to watch."

"How adorable, he wishes for you to watch him parade his skills," Siesta squealed. She quickly pinned my loosely braided fringe back. "Let us go, my lady." She tapped my shoulder to indicate I was ready. I tried to hide my wince but she noticed and pulled back her hand, confused how she had hurt me. Before I could say anything she had pulled away my hair to reveal my injury.

"How did this happen?" she asked seriously.

"We were training this morning and I fell awkwardly, tripping over a log," I said, covering my hair over it once again. I could tell by the look she gave me that she did not believe my words. I walked out the door after the other wolf to dissuade her from any further questions.

Trim instantly followed behind us, Ara at his heels. We walked through the castle grounds into the bright arena. I saw instantly that the training grounds had been set for archery. I looked around at the huge gathering. Many female wolves surrounded us, their hands clutched to their chests in a fawning manner. Awkwardly I held the blue moonstone to my chest. The large mass of wolves was much like an adoring fan club and it took them a minute to notice my entrance. Some of them stepped aside, and when I got to the front, I saw Fimble standing with bow and arrow poised.

He adopted an expression of concentration and then shot his arrow at a straw target strapped to a tree, hitting it dead center. He pulled back another arrow, hitting the center again and almost splitting the first arrow. I watched in amazement. I had not realized he was such a magnificent archer. Perhaps I too was guilty of judging him by his status alone.

Fiesca sat cross-legged, watching over her brother with an expression of boredom. She looked at the other wolves, snarling to herself in disgust at those who fawned over him. His long gray hair lightly moved with the wind. He grabbed another arrow out of the satchel strapped to his back. Although he didn't have a large frame, it was still muscular and taut when he stretched back his arms. He held the bow steady, closing one eye again so he could focus.

Next to him was one of our own talented guards, who dangled a bow dejectedly in his hand as he watched Fimble in awe. I held back the snicker in my throat as he looked so defeated. He was blushing red as he watched in amazement.

I squinted as I tried to follow the arrows' paths, reaching my hand above my eyes to shade them from the sun. All of a sudden it had gotten so bright. I fiddled with my blue moonstone. Everyone else around me seemed unfazed by the brightness and the heat of the sun. I rubbed at my right eye vigorously in an attempt to cleanse it, but to no avail. It must have been aggravated by dust. The sun irritated me so much that I used both hands to shadow my eyes, finding my right one to be particularly affected.

"What is it?" Trim asked me as he noticed my sudden irritation.

"Something is in my eye," I admitted to him. "I think I will go back inside to flush it out with some water." I brushed past him, walking toward the castle again. Clapping erupted behind me. I looked over my shoulder and saw Fimble approach.

He quickly came to my side. "I am so sorry about this morning; I did not mean to let it go on for so long. I did not want to see you attacked so viciously," he blabbed.

"Please do not speak of such matters here," I said, covering my eye and looking behind me to indicate that there were wolves behind us with eager ears.

"My apologies, I was not thinking. Is there something wrong with you eye?" he asked, trying to see through my slim fingers. A hint of panic had edged into his voice.

"No, a bug or something must have flown into it. I was not injured by your sister," I lied. I did not yet know the cause of my injury, but I didn't want others to know that I lacked the skills to protect myself.

"Can I walk you to breakfast? I wish to spend most of the day with you, Sia. Tomorrow there are the celebrations for your eighteenth year. I know you will be busy so I wish to have you for myself most of today," Fimble said forwardly.

"I fear I am not very friendly company today," I said honestly, still with so many thoughts in my mind. I no longer had Siesta's passive, calming voice to take my mind off such matters.

"No matter, I am content in silence, or happy to listen," he said, sincerity shining in his eyes. "I *am* sorry for what happened though, and Trim was right, I should have protected you. I won't let that happen to you ever again. You can depend on me. I will look after you, Sia."

His statement made my stomach tighten and I looked at him with gratitude. It was not awkward to be with him. For someone who was so forward with his words, he made me feel at ease. I even had confidence in his silence; I knew that if I wanted to, I could speak to him about my concerns.

I walked into the shadier parts of the castle and thankfully my eye seemed to flush out the irritation. I blinked rapidly, unsure of what had antagonized it so. Fimble escorted me to the dining area where my parents and his pack were already seated. Trim pulled out my chair and stood back, Ara at his feet.

My mother looked between both Trim and me with concern. I tried to avoid her eyes, still angered by her lies. I felt the burn of Fiesca's eyes on my own also but I did not look up, fearing a repeat of our last encounter in front of my parents. I was not so immature that I would challenge her here at a civilized gathering.

I gathered a few pieces of food onto my plate. There was an awkward silence in the room and only my father and Kratin engaged in light conversation about how their wolves trained and hunted. My father seemed tense as he spoke to Kratin, and his body language was in opposition to the welcoming words he spoke.

There was an uneasiness around the table that not only I felt, but my mother did too. She partook in conversation here and there, but other than that she played with the food on her plate in silence. After a few slow mouthfuls of my own food, I had to sniff it, unsure of what was wrong with it. It did not smell as if the meat had gone off, yet it made me feel sick to my stomach.

I was nauseous as I slowly chewed a few of the vegetables on my plate, avoiding the meat. A sudden bubble stirred in my stomach, making me hold my hand to my mouth firmly. I felt as though I were about to vomit. *But I have been only eating for a few minutes; meat could not poison me so quickly...* I trailed off in thought. I assessed the large slab of meat on the table and then the others who ate theirs without concern.

Trim leaned over my shoulder as I prodded at my plate of food. "Is everything okay?" he whispered in concern. He startled me and my chair screeched back, drawing attention to myself. He straightened up again as everyone looked at us.

Fiesca stopped talking as Fimble turned to me with an expression of concern. "Are you okay?"

I nodded with a light smile, ushering them all away. After a moment of silence everyone began to relax again into their respective conversations, though my mother and father continued to watch me carefully. My stomach turned and I felt violently ill. I motioned for Trim to lower himself beside my chair again so I could whisper into his ear. "I think my meat may be off, it has made me feel terribly ill, but I cannot be certain," I said, raising my hand to my cheek, which felt awfully hot.

He leaned over me, his chest close to my face as he reached for my food. He sniffed it and then looked back at me before raising his hand to my forehead. The acid in my stomach rose up my throat as I tried to hold it down. I turned my face to his stomach so no one else could see the strain on my face. I panted heavily as I fought the urge to empty my stomach.

"Princess Sia is feeling unwell and for the time being she must retreat to her room," Trim announced as he pulled my chair out for me to stand. I stood up lightheadedly. Again my right eye irritated me and I shielded it from the brightness of the flickering flames.

My mother's chair scrapped back, surprising me. She looked so panicked. "I will be okay, Mother, after a few hours' rest," I reassured her. My father gently grasped one of her wrists clutched at her chest to hold her back.

"I will look after her," Trim promised, shielding me from the light of the flickering flames. By the time we had reached my room I was relying on him to walk. He reached out for an unfamiliar bowl that was on my desk and held my hair back as I vomited into it. I shuddered as I coughed up the food, still covering my eye from the bright light shining through my open window. I leaned on the chair for support, too weak to even make my way over to my bed.

"Please block the light," I winced as I hunched over the bowl once again. He seemed hesitant to leave my side and with some reluctance he attended to the window. I was enclosed by darkness. He ushered me onto my bed where I sat on the edge of it, still vomiting.

"I'm here," Trim reassured quietly, pulling back my hair as I panted heavily. I tried to breathe through my pain and panic. My eyes began to water as I slumped forward. My mind rang with Trim's words. *I'm here.* His tone was sincere yet it seemed as though he had stopped himself from saying anything further. If he wasn't so careful with his words perhaps his secret may have slipped, but he had apparently grown too comfortable with his lie. He held my hair and whispered gently to me and I felt as if his words held a significance I could not yet understand.

Chapter Twelve- My Prison

$\mathcal{J}$ was a horrific afternoon that tested the very limits of my endurance. I no longer had food or liquid in my stomach and yet I still hurled. Siesta often came into the room, replacing untouched bowls of food and water with new refreshments that I could not bring myself to touch. Throughout my exhausted retching Trim supported me, holding me up and holding a wet cloth to my hot forehead. Streaks of light that pierced around the edges of the fur that covered the window tortured me. I found myself covering my eye the whole time just in case the sun once again hit it.

I cried and whimpered pathetically as I clung to consciousness. I just wanted to be able to rest, to sleep off such sickness. Every so often I thought of the meat. *Was it deliberately poisoned? Had it merely gone off?* If someone had done this to me on purpose surely there would be an investigation. No one else was sick as they ate. "When you smelled my meat..." I gasped, taking a second to muster the energy to continue. I ran my fingers through my hair as I suddenly thought I might retch. I found Trim's hand already there, supporting my head. Our fingers lingered over one another's briefly before he drew back, allowing me to pull back my own hair. "Did it smell of poison to you?"

"There was nothing wrong with your meat, Sia," he answered carefully.

I furrowed my eyebrows in confusion before hurling once again. My stomach could only empty itself of the small volume of water I had tried to keep down. I crumbled further into myself, no longer able to voice my thoughts. The next few hours were painfully long.

Eventually Siesta took Trim's position by my bedside. I laid my head on her lap, coughing coarsely into the bowl. She dampened my fiery hot skin for me as I held my eye firmly. It now pained me to the extent that I felt like clawing it out.

Trim sat across from me, watching me intently. I could not imagine what he was thinking as he looked at me. My hand shakily rose to my hair as I tried to push a small piece of my fringe away. Siesta quickly brushed it aside for me before pushing my hand back down by my side.

Many hours passed and I knew the sun must have gone down. I panted from exhaustion. I only wanted to rest, yet I could not. My fever rose and I could not speak. My sight grew dim and I pushed heavily on my right eye, trying to exert pressure on it to ease the agitation.

"What is wrong with your eye?" Siesta asked. I could not hide my facial contortions which conveyed my pain. My mouth seemed too dry to speak. I couldn't give her an answer. The pain of it struck me with fear as I had no idea what was happening to me. The vivid images of my dream flashed before my eyes, torturing me in my fever. I recalled the person who wanted to hurt me—how he had stalked me. I curled into myself in fear.

I wondered if my pain was a message, a warning from someone who intended to harm me. I tried to dismiss my pain as a delayed complication from my earlier fight with Fiesca. Memories faded in and out of my consciousness. I focused on the faces of the human man and his sister. *What if this is because I made contact with them? Has this happened because I touched the male? What if….*

As I sobbed I tapped over my eye lightly, as if I were a child pointing to my pain. In my eye there was an excruciating hotness. I pressed down on it, sending shooting pain into it because of the pressure I exerted. I wrapped my black tail around myself, my body aching with hot and cold flushes. Trim stood up as my pain

106

increased in intensity and tapped gently on Siesta's shoulder to indicate that he would take her place.

"Siesta, can you please go and obtain a heavy bandage to wrap over her eye and a light padding to put underneath?" He switched places with her, gently positioning my head on his lap. I curled further into myself and he brushed over my hair lightly as I began to sob.

"Perhaps we should inform the King and Queen?" Siesta enquired.

"They know, please just fetch the bandages. Speak to no one else," Trim ordered. I tried to understand how they could possibly know of the extent of my pain. Neither Trim nor Siesta had so far left my room to report on the severity of my illness. It seemed like his demand that she should speak to no one else held some importance. Could this possibly be something they predicted? I was unable to ask any questions, unable to argue with him.

He fumbled on the small table beside my bed for Lady Momiko's moonstone. Then he pulled my hand away, which made me wince as the brightness of the room suddenly shot through it. He covered it tenderly with the coolness of Lady Momiko's moonstone. I clutched onto it firmly, enjoying some relief, but within seconds my body temperature had heated the stone and it provided me with no further respite from the pain. I winced at the bright lights that pierced my eye, yet I knew my room was dark. I could only partially make out Trim's face, which was cloaked in shadows. No flames had been lit at my request.

Siesta entered my room with the material Trim had asked for. He placed the small cloth against my eye and vigorously wrapped the bandage around my head, covering the patch he had just put on. "Everything will be okay," he said gently, rocking me back and forth as I held my eye firmly. The pain choked me and entrapped me in what felt like a prison. My body felt poisoned.

Was this my death? I dismissed that idea; Trim would never soothe me to sleep if I was in danger of dying.

It was a night of torture as my pain increased. Soon the migraines appeared and my screams began. Thumping began against my sensitive ears like music was being directly played into them. I thought I was losing my mind as I began to hear voices that were not Trim or Siesta's. I cried on Trim's lap, still hurling into the bowl he held beneath me.

Siesta dabbed my face with a cool cloth, looking between both Trim and I frantically. I realized she was as unnerved by his composure as I was. *Why won't my parents come? Why won't Trim tell them of my sudden, grave illness?* My whole body turned and felt as if it were transitioning into death. My eye burned agonizingly and tortured me through the night. It almost compelled me to rip at my own eye. But as I began to try, unable to take such pain anymore, Trim held my hand firmly in his. After that I could get no relief as he no longer let my hand near my eye. He understood my intention. Trim held me firmly, becoming my enemy as he took away my only option for release.

As the night switched over to morning and my body slowly cooled, I thrashed less. My eye felt like it had been gouged and taken; it throbbed heavily. The bandage was my savior as still I felt like everything was too bright for my right eye.

Eventually I could fight no longer as I was physically and emotionally exhausted. I did not know if it was the call of death that enticed me into sleep or another chant I had not heard before. The sounds pulled me into the darkness quickly but I was afforded no respite from the throbbing of my eye while I slept.

Chapter Thirteen- My Seclusion

My giggle echoed throughout the open courtyard. I was six again, innocent and happy. I was pursuing thirteen-year-old Trim through the castle's beautiful, majestic gardens. The flowers of spring had begun to bloom, and their delicate scents filled the air. We both held sticks as we pretended to be fierce fighters. Although his fighting skills were far superior to that of my own— my father had only just begun teaching me how to defend myself—Trim always let me win.

Eventually we collapsed onto the green grass beside one another. We had exhausted ourselves playing games all day. I looked over at Trim, who stared into the sky, deep in thought. My eyes fell upon the unpleasant scar that was left over from the wound that had partially blinded him. At this sensitive age I was only just becoming aware that Trim's face was scary to other wolves.

Curiosity always got the better of me. "Does that side of your face hurt you?" I asked, my cubbish voice still so innocent. Consequences did not yet exist for me. There was nothing to dissuade me from asking the sensitive question.

He raised himself on his elbow, covering his scar as he spoke. "Sometimes... do you think it is ugly?"

"No," I said putting my hands on both sides of his face so he would look at me, instead of away. "Trim is perfect how he looks. Not ugly. Just as long as it doesn't hurt you," I said with a smile. Hesitantly Trim smiled as well.

The scene faded into another memory. By the age of ten we began battling one another seriously. Trim no longer took it easy on me like he once had. He was seventeen and much had changed from our innocent days of play fighting. He now wanted me to be strong, and the play fights were left behind in favor of serious instruction.

His presence by my side was less constant, more sporadic. Trim sometimes left for days. He would go to the woods without mentioning his planned absences. Sometime I was scared. I was terrified he wouldn't come back. At that point he was like a big brother to me. He had been in my life for so long. To have him disappear so suddenly struck fear into my young heart.

I remember once he left for three weeks without one word of warning about his departure. The vivid memory of his return swept through me now in my dream. I was still so small then. I was play fighting with another wolf of my age in the center of the huts. When I looked up, Trim was standing there with many scratches over his body.

I ran to him, arms wide. I hugged him in excitement, just so relieved that he had returned. He patted my head gently. "You were gone for too long this time!" I shouted angrily, pouting as I hugged him tightly.

"I am sorry, Sia," he said. "I will always come back. I promised I would always protect you."

By the age of sixteen, I realized that the innocent days when I merely missed him had vanished. His absence left a hole in my heart. When he departed, even for only a few days, I longed for him. In my sleep I returned to my sixteen-year-old self and experienced how I ached for him as if it were happening all over again. The feeling lingered as my dream faded into a nightmare.

Noises from outside my window encouraged me to sit quietly up in my bed. Shadows streaked the room as the flames flickered. I glanced at the dark shapes, trying to make out if it was Trim or Siesta. As I focused on the corner of the room, I realized there were *two* figures. I took a sharp breath. It was Trim and he was with one of the red-furred wolves from the village, Monique.

"Perhaps if you would consider it, my proposition... you and me?" Monique whispered seductively. I lost my breath at her words, confused as to why I now clutched at my heart. For some reason I instantly hated Monique. Although I had never had any issue with her before, now I *hated* her.

The reality of it hit me. *I think I love Trim.* The thought of another wolf with him burned in my chest painfully. My stomach tightened, making me gasp. The noise startled Ara and she playfully barked at me, wagging her tail happily. I slowly looked up from Ara to the frozen figures. I was terrified that the realization on my face would alert them to the emotions that burned through me. Monique blushed with girlish embarrassment and held her hand to her chest as she coyly excused herself from my presence. I did not hear her words or draw my eyes from Trim's. Monique looked in confusion between us before leaving. We stared at each other for a long moment in the silence, neither of us moving.

I felt lost and confused and without thinking I backed out of the room. I used the walls to support myself as I weakly made for the castle gardens. *Why did I run from him?* I chastised myself.

By the time I had reached the roses, I could hear Trim's steps crunch the gravel of the path behind me. He called out my name. "Sia!" he yelled angrily from behind me. I breathed heavily, trying to contain my shaky emotions. I looked around wildly for another place to run. "Sia, don't ignore me."

"I'm not ignoring you," I defended myself, startled by the tears that trailed down my face. I wrapped my arms around myself. The realization of my love for him made it difficult for me to meet his eye. "You can't go anywhere! You can't go anywhere with... Monique."

"I'm not going anywhere," he quickly reassured me, raising his hands as he approached me.

"I don't know how to look after myself. You promised me that you would look after me forever. How can you if you have a family?" I babbled. I knew I was being selfish but the words were running off my tongue.

"Sia, I am not leaving," he breathed out quickly. His voice was raw with emotion. "I won't leave your side." He looked deep into my eyes as he said it. I frantically looked him up and down in confusion, breathing raggedly. "Come here."

I only paused for half a second before walking into his arms and accepting the warmth of his embrace. I clung desperately to him and he held me just as passionately. I had always wanted to have him so close. He rested his chin between my perked ears as I cried into his chest. So many times as a child I had done this, but now it held far more significance. I knew now I *needed* him.

The harsh realization that I was only dreaming penetrated the inner recesses of my mind and my eyes quickly opened into the darkness. I was torn away from the fantasy my mind had created in its feverish state and transported into sudden, painful reality. All warmth from his touch left my skin and the cruel cold reawakened me to my suffering. I lay in the darkness, my eyes wide open as I faced my feelings.

It had been a long time since he had been as open with me as he had been in my dream, and even longer since he had held me in his arms. I had desperately tried to impress him in training as I grew older. I engaged in combat like a woman, not a cub. I wanted to prove to him who I was, who I could be. I began to wear more gems and tie my hair differently. But the more I attempted to engage his attention, the more he distanced himself.

The last time he was so close to me was when I was sixteen, and he had extricated himself from my embrace. He then turned cold and kept himself at a distance. We began to talk less and less and his tone took a lecturing, scornful edge. I had known Trim when he was playful and kind, but in those two years, much had changed. *We* had changed.

I had found myself far more curious about the outside world. I also took my training seriously. I wanted to defend myself. Although my heart tore for him, I put the gems away and only styled my hair the one way. I began to run and found that he would always chase. I had both Trim's interest and my freedom when I fled from my royal status. From those years of being a cub much had changed and in my darkest thoughts I worried that we had both changed far too much. The differences in our ages had led us down separate paths.

I felt now that I was only a mere promise he had made a long time ago; that I held no more value to him than keeping an oath he had made to Sia, the Phantom Wolf.

I shifted uncomfortably in my bed, exhausted by the scope of emotions I had been forced to confront. My mouth was dry and my head felt numb from the dreams. My body felt like it had been beaten to near death and I hesitated to move, even if I could. It was dark and my room was clouded with an eerie atmosphere.

I moved my fingers enough to brush the familiar fur of Ara, who must have been by my side the whole night. My right eye still pounded heavily as I used my left to focus on the figure in the corner of my room. His blue eye shone back at me, just as it always did. Trim remained still as he watched me. Siesta was no longer in the room.

Trim slowly stood up and walked to my bedside table, where the water was. He rested one hand gently beneath my head as he raised the water to my lips. I gulped slowly, although I was so parched my stomach churned at its contact with the cool water.

He placed it back down, looking at my patched eye as I looked at his scarred one. I wanted to ask him what had happened to me, why he was so calm amongst all that had happened. I knew it was not a normal illness; I knew something so sudden and rash was not normal. And yet the way he acted suggested that he had somehow predicted what would happen. I thought of the bowl that was already conveniently placed on my table when we raced back to my room; it was not usually there. It seemed too much of a coincidence that it had been positioned there just as I had fallen ill. Even though he had helped me and looked after me all through the traumatic night, I knew he was still lying to me.

He walked back to his chair and sat down. He leaned forward so that his chin rested against his clasped hands, his elbows on his strong legs. I felt his steady eye on me, like always, just watching. A tear streamed down my left eye when I thought of the gifts he had offered me only yesterday—the moonstones at my chest, the morning run. Did he anticipate this and feel sorry for me?

Today was my eighteenth birthday and yet I wallowed in pain and misery. I didn't want to see anyone, even if it was in my power to physically move. I grinded my teeth in frustration, tasting my own blood as my canines slightly lengthened. I raised my tongue to them but they hadn't moved. I was surprised by what I had thought I had felt. *What has happened to me?*

*

For a few days I would not allow anyone in my room. I barred my parents from entering as I felt they had betrayed me so much. They respected my wishes as they did not want to distress me while I was recovering. I recalled the look that was exchanged between Trim and my mother as they stood in the doorway. My father held her back from coming to my side. I could not shake the suspicion that they had known this would happen.

I wouldn't allow Siesta to spend any time in my room but allowed her to take Ara out to be fed and walked. Trim would not leave my room. We were both like statues that weathered in the rain. Unmoving, silent, devoid of emotion—eroding.

Slowly I regained the sensation of my senses and a command over my body. My eye still throbbed and I was unable to adapt to the dark room. Everything felt too bright. Although I could move I chose not to, the darkness consumed me and I only wanted to stay in my room. I was unable to climb their mountain of lies.

"We cannot stay in here forever, Sia," Trim said, his voice raw as it broke the bitter silence. The air was so still that the words seemed to soak the air. I ignored him, wishing he too had left my side days ago. "Your parents are worried about you."

"You all lied to me," I said, my voice sounding a lot more pained than I had intended.

"It is not as you see it—"

"Not how I *see* it? I cannot see out of one of my eyes!" I shouted, raising myself in my bed angrily. I winced at the pain of moving so quickly after days of no movement. I cowered into myself, clutching at my stomach—it felt as if I were recovering from a stab wound.

After much silence I looked at him. His one eye looked back at me from his expressionless mask. For most of his life now he had only the sight of his left eye. I held back the tears from my eyes. To look at him pained me. If I could not trust my own parents and Trim—who had looked after me all my life—then whom could I trust?

"I know, and I am sorry," he said with sympathy, kneeling by my side. He looked to the ground before looking up at me with his one eye.

"I cannot trust you," I told him honestly. I wept as the truth of the words pained me so much. Still, he gave me no answers; still, he lied to my face. He had apologized, but I didn't know if that was for breaking my trust or what had happened to me.

"I know. I will build your trust again. I have always been here to protect you. And right now, you may not see it as I do, but you will understand I have only ever lied to protect you," he said, slowly standing, his shoulder widening as he stretched.

"If that is still how you wish to treat me, then I cannot be near you anymore. I will not be treated in such a way. You do not know what is best for me," my voice shook as I spoke the truthful words. I had always felt there was distance between Trim and me, but this was the furthest I had been pushed. It was no longer healthy for me to have him so close after he had given me a lifetime of lies.

"No, but I have pledged my life to protect you. Whether you want me near or not, I will still be there. For now, Sia, we need to go outside, much has happened during your absence. There was much disappointment when you did not arrive for your own festivities. Your mother has not eaten for days because she is so worried about you. I give you no choice in this any longer; you are starting to resemble a corpse."

He moved over to the fur that hung over my window and ripped it down. I whimpered against the wall next to my bed, hiding my face as my right eye instantly burned. I held it firmly, almost in tears at the pain. "What is this? What have you done to me?" I whimpered.

"I don't know what has happened to your eye, Sia, but let us clean your body and assess it, shall we?" he asked, holding his hand out to me. I braved myself to face the bright light as I struggled to stand on my own feet, unwilling to accept his help. *I cannot rely on Trim anymore.*

As I stood my ankle rolled and I fell into Trim clumsily. I was agitated by my weak body and I pushed him away so that I was only holding myself up by his arm. "I will not leave this room if I can't walk on my own!" I said, angry at both him and my body.

He only looked at me with his expressionless face before grabbing Lady Momiko's stick, which was next to my bedside table. He offered it to me but I looked at it as if it were an omen. He persisted so I reluctantly took it. I steadied my weight on it as I started slowly walking by myself. My hand tightly clutched around the stick. I was infuriated by the realization that Lady Momiko may have foreseen this. I had asked myself so many times why she had gifted me with her stick, and now in my weakened state, I was forced to use it.

"Have we found Lady Momiko yet?" I asked. I began to realize she had foreseen my illness and I wondered if her disappearance was somehow connected. If something were to happen, she would take the right precautions. Perhaps she has left for a purpose without telling anyone else.

"No, we haven't yet," Trim admitted as we walked from my room and up the stairs. I led myself with my sensitive hearing, not wanting anyone to see me in such a weak state. Much to my surprise my hearing was exceptional, more so than it had ever been. I pinned my ears back, slightly confused as I could even hear the distant chopping of wood. *Impossible.*

"Sia?" Trim asked, snapping me out of my trance.

I looked ahead, unable to hear anyone in the bathing chambers. I slowly began walking again, though I kept looking into the direction that I had distinctly heard the chopping of wood. *Has my hearing sharpened?* I tried to push such imaginative thoughts away, blaming it on the days spent in silence. *My ears are only sensitive as I haven't heard much noise lately,* I tried to convince myself. But as we walked into the bathing chambers I realized I was proved right—there was no one there.

The tub I usually bathed in only had cool water in it as the wood beneath had already burned out. But it was not the bathing itself I had come for, but to see my reflection. I walked up to one of the large mirrors, taking in my weak, feeble body. My face had been bandaged up.

Slowly I peeled the bandage from around my head, fearful of what it might reveal. Perhaps nothing, but my instinct told me to prepare myself. Trim watched me carefully from a distance as I unwrapped the bandage, eventually revealing the small padding. I hesitated as I raised my hand to it. I pulled it away, my hand instantly losing its grip on the stick that held me up. I dropped to the floor, panting heavily at my ugliness. Trim came down to my side and rested his hand on my back, letting me know I was not alone. My right eye was no longer blue; it had now turned green. *This was not my eye.*

"It isn't mine," I echoed my thoughts shakily. Trim grabbed my cheeks to properly assess it. I saw in his eye that he was also frightened. He dropped back, slumping beside me against the wall. He was breathing harshly as he ran his fingers through his disarrayed orange hair.

It only alarmed me further to see his reaction. Trim, who was never unnerved or frightened, was undoubtedly flustered. He rubbed at his jaw, vigorously assessing my face. Both our ears flattened as we heard two wolves approach. Trim quickly grabbed the bandage and dressed my eye again, frightening me with his urgency. He hurriedly tightened it, hurting me slightly.

"You mustn't show or tell anyone of this," he said whilst leaning over me and cupping my face. I placed my hands over his, feeling like a bewildered child.

"What is it? What is wrong with me?" My voice lowered as I heard the others come toward us. *What terrible thing has happened that I have to be sworn to secrecy?*

118

"I don't know. I need to verify with your parents. Only they will know." He released his hold of me just before the two female wolves entered, gossiping to one another. They stopped as they noticed us, both of us breathing heavily as we looked back up at them. They dropped their heads as if they had witnessed something they shouldn't have. I looked down at my ruffled state and blushed as if I were guilty. I wondered if they had seen him holding me so closely and fiercely. *Do they think we were having a passionate moment?*

I once fantasized about such a thing happening, that we would have a secret to share; that he would fiercely grab me, awakened by a sudden desire or longing for me. But now those days seemed far behind me. Trim had dropped his walls in front of me. He had shown me his fear. This change in my eye had unsettled him to his core.

"Princess Sia, I apologize, we did not know you were feeling well again," one of the wolves said timidly. Her mouth opened and closed, as if she wanted to ask something, but didn't. Her companion was not quite so reserved, "My, what has happened to your eye?"

I looked at Trim, unable to think on the spot about how to respond.

"Princess Sia has caught a terrible bug, it has infected her eye. She must bandage it for many days, even weeks, as it may take her sight," Trim said, now collected. "Please do not speak of this to anyone for the time being, it is a sensitive topic to both her and her parents. I am sure you understand."

"Of course, my apologies for asking and I hope you fare well soon, Princess Sia," the red-haired wolf said. I looked at him, abashed at how quickly and easily he could lie. *How many lies has he fed me with such ease?*

Trim supported me until he had retrieved Lady Momiko's walking stick. Using it, I walked past the two wolves with as much dignity as I could muster as I went in search of my parents. My keen hearing already alerted me to their presence in the library.

We walked away from the wolves until they were no longer in hearing distance. I grabbed his arm with the all the strength I could gather, pulling him back. "Please Trim, I beg of you, whatever you think it is you see, please tell me," I pleaded with him. He looked away from my intense stare. "Please?" I whispered gently. Surely he could not keep something of this importance from me. I recalled the reflection of my face with the two mismatched eyes. If everyone looked at me with the same fear that filled his eyes when he saw me then I could not handle such an existence. I needed to know what it was he saw.

"I think... " he said looking away from me and burrowing his eyebrows over his eyes in confusion. "I think it is a Phantom Wolf's eye."

My grip loosened on him. *How is such a thing possible? How could that possibly be? I was not killed by a human... I do not have the sudden urge to kill my pack...*

"We need to go to your parents," he said, grabbing my hand and pulling me slowly along to the library.

I was too shocked to even respond. *How is it even possible that I could have the eye of a Phantom Wolf?*

Chapter Fourteen- Attachment

$\mathscr{I}$hobbled along to the library, silent as I reflected on how my parents might react. I wasn't sure how they would be able to confirm that I even had a Phantom Wolf's eye. I dreaded having the discussion. It occurred to me once again that they might even have predicted this.

Trim opened the door for me and gently helped me inside. My parents looked grave when they saw my weakened state. "Oh Sia!" my mother wailed as she ran over to me. "I am so sorry." She hugged me tightly, her light-brown ears pinned back as she cried into my neck. I hovered my hand over her back, surprised by her sudden outburst.

"I will stay outside on watch in case someone approaches," Trim said politely as he edged out of the room. "You have much to say." He closed the door behind me and we stood in momentary silence.

My father took my arm to support me over to the couch before carefully settling me against the cushions. "What is wrong with your eye?" he asked worriedly. It was the most noticeable of my injuries; of course it would be the first question he would ask.

"I... I don't know," I honestly said, as I slowly began to unwrap it. "I think it may be better if you saw it for yourselves." I unwrapped the bandage as my parents looked on in suspense. They gasped as I removed the padding from my green eye.

My mother's hand flew to her mouth, prompting my father to place a reassuring hand on her shoulder while he carefully looked into my eye. In my right eye everything was much brighter. My eyesight was much keener; it even seemed at times that the floating dust particles irritated me as they fell in front of my eye.

"What is wrong with me?" I asked quietly while I patiently waited for them to regain their composure. "Am I going to die?"

"No. No, you will not," my mother stated with determination. "Saith?" She looked up at him questioningly, desperate for him to confirm her words.

I thought of Trim and his behavior throughout my ordeal. *Is this what Trim thought them to know?* It appeared they thought of him at the same time as I did.

"Have you shown Trim this?" my father asked me, looking back at the door. I knew Trim would be within hearing distance of this conversation and it unnerved me that it was the first question my father would ask. I could only nod in answer.

"He has suspicions it might be a Phantom Wolf's eye," I exhaled. I desperately wanted them to refute his suspicions. "But... that is not possible, that cannot be?" I had intended my denial to come out as a statement, rather than a question, but I needed them to soothe me. To become a Phantom Wolf you must first be killed by a human. And when you awaken from your death you are cursed as a Phantom Wolf. You slaughter your pack. But none of that had happened to me.

"It is not just a Phantom Wolf's eye," my father said in contemplation. He looked back at my mother who nodded in confirmation. "It has a very distinctive resemblance to *Sia's* eyes."

My ears itched as I heard Trim shuffling uncomfortably behind the door. "Sia, the last Phantom Wolf?" I asked, turning to look behind me at the large painting of my uncle Kiba and his lover. Sia's vivid green eyes shone back at me from the portrait. "That is not possible."

"Lady Momiko told us only a few months ago that you were to fall gravely sick upon your eighteenth birthday. She swore us to secrecy so we could not take away your innocence leading up to it. But that is all she told us; she did not tell us what could have caused such an illness," my father said while staring into my mismatched eyes.

I was dumbfounded as I thought of Lady Momiko. I could only fiddle with the moonstone at my chest as I remembered her words. She had announced she had three gifts to give me, but she had only given me two. Was this the intended third?

"So you let me go through this pain, even though you knew it would happen and you could have warned me," I confirmed. I was beyond hurt that they remained silent when they could have somehow prevented me from my suffering. "How do I get rid of it?"

"Sia, we do not know," my mother said mournfully. "Does it hurt you?"

"I was in that room for so many days. On the first I wanted to rip my own eye out," I replied. "My body aches, and it feels as though I am recovering from death itself. And now I find out you have known all this time and you did not have the slightest inclination to tell me. So, my dear mother, my eye is not the only thing that is hurt."

"It is not your mother's fault. We were sworn to secrecy; it is not as if we didn't want to speak of this to you," my father interjected, defending my mother.

"And what of the pack? Why are they here? Will you tell me now?" I demanded.

I struggled to concentrate on the conversation at hand. In my right eye everything seemed too bright. My eye was raw and sensitive, and the other seemed as though it were shadowed in darkness in comparison. Without my bandage a migraine had started to pulse from the contrast in light. The anger that built within me was quick and temperamental, like I might attack my own parents in anger. I almost felt as if I could not control it; that it consumed me completely. I pushed the thought from my mind that perhaps my rage was enhanced because of my Phantom Wolf eye. Those who were cursed were often known to struggle with controlling their murderous instinct; had my body truly changed in such a way?

"Lady Momiko's foresight allowed us to understand that we must keep them close—that they are a threat and we have to monitor them closely. She explained that soon everything would make sense. She has told us to prepare ourselves, but we could tell no one in the Kingdom as we do not know who we can trust. Not everyone is aligned with us as we had first thought, but we do not know who. She was not shown their faces," my father explained as his shoulders dropped in exhaustion. He had gushed the truthful words, obviously guilt-ridden. "She told us the only way we could draw them here was to propose your entwinement with one of Kratin's sons; just as she has foretold, they have come."

I thought of Trim's sudden interest in staying by my side, never leaving me alone even for one moment. This had been predicted, and I was the only one who was kept in the dark as disaster fell not only upon myself but upon my pack and home.

"You blindly allowed yourself to be guided by Lady Momiko, who is no longer here. Now what will you do?" I asked seriously. We had delved into something we did not understand, guided only by prediction rather than fact. How could they rely so heavily on an instinct that could so easily be wrong?

My parents were silent as they dropped their gaze to the floor.

"For now, Trim is to stay close to you. We will continue as if we haven't had this discussion because the pack is still here. For whatever reason it is, Lady Momiko wanted that pack here. She has helped us and guided us for many years, we must believe in her," my father finally said, his confidence building with each word.

"And what of this?" I asked, almost crying as I pointed to my eye. I grasped firmly onto the handle of Lady Momiko's stick. "Am I to be cursed with this forever? Or is that something else we will wait to find out?"

"We will find a cure for it, but we do not know it happened," my mother said faintly. I crumbled slowly into my chair, watching as my mother slowly turned even paler. Her body was so fragile. She often lost consciousness if she was too stressed or if she was confronted by undesirable images.

"When Trim saw this eye, he feared me. If others see this eye, I fear they will be just as stricken. I know how other wolves regard Phantom Wolves. They are to be feared and avoided," I said, my voice trailing as I recalled all the stories that my parents had told me: the villages that would not accept them, those who hunted them, the self-destruction they forced on themselves because they could not live with such a lonely existence.

Phantom Wolves were connected to that murderous human responsible for their curse; hand-in-hand, their lives were entwined. I thought of the human I had made contact with, and then I remembered the sudden urge Trim had to take me for a walk that very day. Had Lady Momiko told him to take me for a walk—was it already foreseen that I would meet with that human? Could he have done this to me? Was mere physical contact all that was needed to be cursed?

"My sweet, I do not think it is the eye he feared but the memories connected with whom it belonged to," my mother said compassionately. I looked into her sad eyes and thought of how much pain she must be in. It was her best friend's eye I was now bearer to. Although it was only theory alone, when I looked back at the painting of the mighty Phantom Wolf, whom I was named after, I couldn't help but believe that it may be true.

I replaced the padding over my eye and began bandaging it once again to protect me from the brightness; already the migraine had pushed me into a fever. I could not adjust to the use of my right eye so quickly.

Ara barked suddenly from outside of the room, where she sat faithfully next to Trim. My ears pinned back as I heard footsteps quickly approach. Just as I had fully concealed my eye, Trim opened the door and closed it hastily behind him. Ara ran ahead of him and jumped on my lap. His eye quickly swept over my own, making sure it was covered. "I am sorry to interrupt but someone is coming. For now I believe we should claim that Sia has contracted an infection after a bug flew into her eye. She cannot reveal it to anyone."

"You are as rational and clever as always, Trim," my father said, placing his hand on Trim's shoulder and nodding to him in acknowledgment. "Thank you for looking after my daughter."

Trim nodded at him gravely just as the wooden doors of the room opened. We all glanced up as Siesta made her entrance. Her body language was apologetic for the interruption, but her tone was urgent. "If I may speak?" she said quickly from near the door. After gaining approval she did so, "It is Lady Momiko; she has made an appearance in the village again. She even greeted the foreign pack before we could escort her back to her room. She looks much worse than she did before she left. But she wishes for no one to visit her."

My mouth widened at the old wolf's sudden appearance. What was she plotting? We had purposefully tried to hide her whereabouts because of the suspicious interest that pack had in her. Or had she already known? I stood, flushed. I was eager to speak with her at once, regardless of her wishes. Even if she did not want to have me as a visitor, I needed answers that it seemed only she could give. I forgot my lack of strength and I fell awkwardly into my father. Both he and Trim instantly moved to catch me.

I closed my eyes in frustration. *Why will my body not act according to my will? Why can I not even stand properly?* I raged inwardly. I eyed her stick suspiciously— she had seen far enough into the future to know that all of this would happen to me. What else was she hiding?

"I will take Sia now to rest," Trim confirmed with my father. Before I could argue he shot me a stern look. "Whatever is coming, and whatever Lady Momiko has foreseen, I think you should be rested for it."

I looked over at Siesta as she patiently waited for me. Her look was one of pity as I began to slowly hobble out of the room. She took my arm gently and we began our slow journey to my room.

Trim was right. Whatever was coming must be big, and before it, I should rest so that I could protect not only myself, but the others as well.

Chapter Fifteen- Hidden Intent

I was once again in the library, unescorted and without Ara. I was alone and the room was dark; The Great Phantom Wolf's green eyes shone down on me from the painting. I was drawn to the fireplace and I moved further into the room, my eyes on the hypnotizing, dancing flames.

The streak of a shadow caught my eye as it flashed past me. I looked around the room, frightened that I was being stalked by the wolf of my previous dream. I steadied myself, firmly using Lady Momiko's stick to stand on my own.

Whispers began to stir in the room and my ears pinned back in uncertainty. I tried to narrow my hearing on the words. "Who's there?" I demanded as the whispers continued to encircle me. Suddenly Lady Momiko's voice rang out as clearly as a light shining in a dark room. I grasped onto her familiar, sharp voice.

"That was not my third gift, child, but a gift to you from another," she said, her words forcing me to straighten my back in surprise. I stumbled as I took a step back and fell backward into a bookshelf. I reached to support myself on a shelf and when I leaned my weight onto it, it twisted to one side. Losing my balance I fell against the bookshelf, but somehow landed on dirty ground. When I had finished coughing I realized I was now entrapped in a dark room. My right eye could dimly determine my surroundings. Even though I knew I was in complete darkness, the vision in my green eye was so enhanced that I could still see ahead of me. I looked into the long, narrow, dirty hallway. Behind me the bookshelf had closed, locking me out of the library.

A secret hallway?

A screeching noise began irritating my sensitive ears. I pulled on them as the noise intensified, trying to block the maddening pitch. Bats swarmed me as I screamed helplessly into the darkness.

*

I sat upright in my bed, panting harshly and clutching my right eye. The pain had grown worse since that morning. Siesta sat beside me with a cool cloth to my face. I was hot and sweaty from the distress of my dream. I burrowed my eyebrows in thought as Siesta spoke to me.

Was it a message? Is there a room behind one of the bookshelves near the fireplace? I thought of Lady Momiko's words. She had stated she had not yet given me my third gift. But *what* was from another? My hand flew to my eye—could it possibly be considered a *gift*? Siesta's speech came to me in fragments and I nodded my head politely. My curiosity burned. I had been shown a secret room and now I needed to know where it would lead. *I must have been shown it so I would investigate it*, I thought to myself. And somewhere deep within my stomach I instinctively felt that I was right.

I looked toward the door, knowing that Trim would not allow it—but I could not dismiss such a powerful pull. I *needed* to find that room. I explored the ways in which I could escape from his attention, rejecting idea after idea. Suddenly I grabbed Siesta's arm as the thought came to me.

"Siesta, could you get me a heavily flavored, scented hot drink; and place some herbs in it that will make me sleep. The smell upsets my stomach but I really need my rest. I need it to be able to sleep," I said innocently, my mind on my devious plan. "Oh, please also bring another normal hot drink for Trim; it must be so tiresome guarding me this closely."

"Of course, my lady," she said with a smile, handing the cloth to me. As she left I wiped my face over with the cloth. If Trim would drink the potion then within mere minutes he would be sound asleep. He would be heavily sedated for an hour, two at most.

I *had* to explore the filthy hall and find out where it would lead. My skin crawled with the same coolness I felt in my dream. Down that hall was an eeriness I could not shake, and I knew someone had tried to lead me there.

As requested Siesta brought in the two drinks, indicating to me which one was mine. I was happy to note that the heavily sedated one smelled no different to the other, and should therefore not arouse Trim's suspicions. When Siesta looked away briefly I swapped them around, collecting the normal one for myself.

I held out to her the other steaming mug. "Would you please offer this to Trim?" She took the cup and began to cross the room. I could hear him shuffling about outside my door, tirelessly guarding me. I felt dishonest for using such methods, but then I recalled the many times before that he had done the exact same thing to me—put me to sleep so I would not try to sneak out at night or in the early morning. I hesitated no further. "Also, I think Ara may need to go for a short walk."

I tapped Ara under the face with my foot, lifting her slightly to wake her, and she sat up sleepily. Siesta called for her to go for a walk. Ara cocked her head to the side, looking at me in confusion. I motioned for her to go with Siesta.

I waited for a couple of minutes, focusing my keen hearing on Trim's movements. With satisfaction I soon realized he had been successfully tricked into drinking the cup of herbs. I used Lady Momiko's stick to stand. The moonstone she gifted me was shining with a dim light. I picked it up and turned it over in my hand. I could use this for light instead of a flame. I could not push

130

aside the idea that she had given me the means to see in darkness for a certain purpose.

I walked past Trim as he peacefully slept in his slumped position. He looked so calm. Sleep deprived him of the opportunity to set his face into his usual scornful expression. He even looked young. His disposition when awake aged him and he appeared much older than he was. Sometimes it was hard to imagine the age gap was as small as it was. We were only divided by seven years and yet at times it felt like a lifetime. He still treated me as a cub. I paused a second longer to consider his youthful face. The age difference was inconsequential to me because of the depth of my feelings. But now, after so many lies, I couldn't confirm with myself if I still desired a future with him.

I listened out for anyone ahead. I was distracted by the sounds of clashing weapons. The archery skills of wolves were once again being paraded to an adoring crowd. No sounds emanated from the hallway, confirming that I could easily walk up to the library without being detected. As I began to sneak past Trim, Ara barked at me and came to my side. I looked at her in surprise. She had run away from Siesta in search of me. Often I thought Ara was too clever.

I hurriedly walked up the stairs and opened the door carefully to the library. I had to make sure no one was in the library, and, for once, my mother was not there. I supposed she was taking part in the welcoming ceremony for the new cub with the other women. We walked inside, the moonstone shining dimly and guiding our path. I approached the fireplace that had now turned into a pile of ash.

The room contained an eclectic collection of wooden, antique bookshelves that lined the walls. My mother was an avid reader and that was known throughout the Kingdom. Wolves presented to her with intricate, ornate furniture as a token of their loyalty. My eyes fell upon the exact bookshelf from my dream. I pushed carefully down on the shelf, but nothing budged. I raised

131

the moonstone to the spines of the books, sure that this was the bookshelf I had fallen through. I examined the dusty collection of books that dated back for decades. As I looked at all the handwritten titles on the spines of the books I noticed one title was written by my father. His calligraphy was unmistakable; his style was unique and admired by many.

I went to pull it out, intrigued as to what kind of book my father had written. It only slightly budged, and instead the bookshelf opened like a door. I coughed hysterically at all the dust that swarmed around my face, causing Ara to sneeze too. The long, dark hall seemed to howl with an eerie wind. There was no light and a lingering, stale smell. From a quick glance I could see a few paintings of our ancestors on the wall. Some were tattered and torn as if someone had ripped at them, others were intact but dusty. I looked behind me to make sure no one had followed. I had left the door slightly ajar so that I could escape if necessary. I had to be quick so no one would notice that I had even opened the door.

I used Lady Momiko's moonstone as guidance as I cautiously walked into the darkness. I was on edge as if I was expecting something to jump out at me, but nothing did. More paintings emerged as I traveled further into the hallway. They were similar to the ones of our ancestors that decorated the walls of the castle.

I began to discern the shape of an opened door. Using the moonstone I saw that there were two wooden doors, their metal hinges slightly rusted. I pushed open the one that was already slightly ajar. It was a heavy door and it creaked loudly as it gave way. I slipped inside, blinking in the darkness. My eyes adjusted to the blackness and I determined an impressively sized chair that took center stage in the middle of the room. It was undoubtedly the throne of a king, or at least someone of royal office. Tall sticks encircled its perimeter. Once they would have been used to light up the room brightly. I swung my moonstone to my left and gasped at a moving figure. It paused as I did, and as I stepped closer and squinted I saw that it was only my reflection in a large mirror. Nostalgia erupted inside me. I couldn't fight the feeling that I had once looked at it before.

The room was so far silent but suddenly I became aware of slow build-up of noise. Too frightened to turn around, I peered over the shoulder of my reflection, but the moonstone was not bright enough to afford me much sight. I turned around slowly, my heart pounding. The clattering around me seemed to rise and fall, yet I could ascertain no other being in the room. Scuffled sounds nearby indicated a fight was taking place. I stepped forward into the direction of the noise, but the room was empty.

All I heard was the beating of my heart and my ragged breaths as a heavy silence descended yet again. My heart rate slowed and I swallowed anxiously. The silence was too heavy—haunting, even. My ears pulled back as a woman's voice pierced the silence with a whisper that seemed to echo around me. *"I loved your brother,"* the voice reverberated. I was disorientated but I looked ahead to where I imagined the voice might have come from. Using my instinct and intensified hearing I was able to imagine that some wolves—some *spirits*—were caught in a terrible reenactment of death. The atmosphere was thick with a powerful energy. The woman's words swirled round me, fragmented at times and unbearably loud at others. In my mind I could see figures, one held captive. One figure bit into the ear of the other before tearing it off. I understood what had happened without seeing it. The noises and voices I heard were enough for me to envision the actions of the shadowed figures.

Many sounds erupted around me, gaining in intensity. As if there were a flicker of lightning, the room was lit up with life and for a split second I was transported to the scene before being cloaked in darkness yet again. There were many wolves in the room when this event occurred. I gasped in terror and stumbled backwards, my hand pressing onto the cold surface of the mirror. I turned from my vision and placed both hands onto the mirror, looking downwards as I gasped for breath.

The energy of the room was palpable. Slowly, I raised my eyes to my reflection. My heart stopped and I jolted back. Sia, the deceased Phantom Wolf, looked back at me from the mirror. She also stepped back, her green eyes stared dimly into mine, imploring me to understand. My hands flew to my eye and I breathed shakily into my clasped hands. I lowered my hands as I caught my breath. Sia was now positioned on her knees before me with many weapons protruding from her back. Her eyes held mine for half a second longer before she fell to the ground. Instantly the image and her spirit disappeared, as if that was all they wanted to show me. The atmosphere became peaceful once again and the silence more natural. I blinked vigorously before rubbing at my right eye. It had responded oddly to the scene before me. The pain seemed to intensify, and blotches of bright light flashed, forcing me to step back unsteadily. It created a dizzy sensation in my mind as my stomach curled. It were as if I had revisited my own memory of pain.

I realized when I studied the cement floor further that this room had witnessed the deaths of many wolves. There was dry blood everywhere, yet it was without an odor. Someone had tried to clean it; some brush marks were still evident where they had scrubbed vigorously.

The realization dawned on me that this was the scene of Sia's death. This was the very place where she had killed my uncle Taleb; where she had killed the human to whom she was connected; where her life had ended. Somehow I was no longer frightened. I stood still in the dark, eerie room, trying to absorb what I had seen. *How is it even possible for me to see such things?* As if giving me an answer, the moonstone glowed magnificently in my hand. I looked at it in amazement.

I looked around the room again, wondering if I had been summoned to such a place and made to witness such a scene so that I would be aided in using her eye—if in fact this was her eye. I raised my hand to my eye, which was still heavily bandaged, wondering if Sia had cursed me with it. She out of all wolves knew the repercussions of having such a curse inflicted upon you. My right eye no longer hurt as much as it once had. Something had provided it with relief since entering the room.

I thought of the time before my birth when my father and mother first began to reign over this kingdom, which had since grown tremendously. Did they purposefully hide this room because of the terrible memories it brought back? I could certainly fathom how the room would produce feelings too raw to face.

A streak of white caught my eye. I went to the mirror, kneeling in front of it while avoiding the spot on the floor that was stained with Sia's blood. I stared at myself in the mirror. Wind blew through my hair and once again my attention was grabbed by something white caught in my hair. I ran my fingers through the strands of my tangled hair, pausing as I realized what I had seen there was a large streak of white in the underlay of my hair.

I recollected the stories. Once a Phantom Wolf was cursed their fur turned to dead white. I touched the white strands in amazement. All signs led to the assumption that somewhere within me I was undergoing a transformation—I was part Phantom Wolf.

Ara barked causing me to jump out of my skin. I looked over at the doors, if only to reassure myself I could escape at any time. But I saw I was not alone. Fimble looked back at me, his eyes sad. I tucked away the white part of my hair, it would only create suspicion.

"Fimble?" I said, surprised I had not noticed or heard him creeping up on me. I must have been really absorbed by my theories. I looked around stupidly, already knowing we were alone. Why was he here? I remembered my parents' warning about the foreign pack and their caution that we pretend not to know of anything ominous.

"Are you okay?" he asked, looking around the room. He seemed to surprise himself with the question. He slowly began to come closer to my seated position beside the mirror. Ara stood next to me, on guard, but she did not growl or bark, which was not characteristic of her. Usually she was quite vocal in the presence of new people or around people she thought untrustworthy.

"I am feeling much better," I said, trying to keep my composure. I used Lady Momiko's stick to stand, noticing I was no longer as reliant on it for support as I once was. I observed that the aches in my body were slowly diminishing. I felt as if I had been gathered in some sort of warmth which gradually replenished me. I looked at the room again, almost certain now that this was a place I was meant to see.

"So, this is the room where all their fates led them?" Fimble asked, his tone foreign. I could see him thinking, contemplating. I feared he was considering whether he should attack me or not. If my father was right then this was the perfect time and place for one of them to attack me. My stomach turned at the thought. I could not imagine that Fimble would try to hurt me.

"I just found it," I said, hiding Lady Momiko's moonstone behind my back. He noticed my distrust and his eyes took on a quality of sadness. He held his hands behind his back, so I could not see them. His face tore with confusion and I saw that he trembled. I readied myself for his attack, certain he was concealing a weapon behind his back.

He revealed the knife to me, causing Ara to growl and snarl at him. I was saddened. I had thought him kind-hearted and good and now I could see he was not that wolf after all.

136

"I'm sorry," he said, looking as if he were about to cry. "I can't do it."

He threw the blade across the room and then crouched with his head in his hands. He rubbed over his face while I looked between him and the blade, unsure of what had happened.

"I don't understand," I said looking between the two. But wasn't he here to attack me? To kill me?

Suddenly he sprang to his feet and came cautiously toward me. I took a few steps back in alarm, bumping against the mirror behind me. I raised Lady Momiko's stick to him as a weapon. My heart raced as I realized the gravity of the position I was in.

"We need to leave... We need to leave the castle now," he said breathlessly.

"You came here to kill me!"

"I can explain it all to you soon, right now we need to find your parents and warn them. My pack... they are here to kill you all..." he explained, stretching out his hands to me. I stared into his eyes—all the kind words he had offered me; the impression I had of him; the rose he had plucked for me. All a lie. *Everything was a lie.*

"Get away from me," I said pivoting around him. I walked forward toward the door, Lady Momiko's stick clenched in my hand. My legs were now strong enough that I could walk unsupported. I left him in the darkness and broke out into a run in the dark hallway. My stamina was not what it usually was and I slumped against the walls as I escaped from the gloomy room.

When I broke out into the hotter air of the library, my ears pulled back as I realized a wolf was on my right. I raised my stick to his blade, knocking it out of his hand. It was one of the archers who had accompanied Fimble. He jumped on me and a scream ripped from my lips in surprise. His claws rose to my face, but a dagger hit him in the side of the head, keeling him over. I stood open-mouthed in shock. I just watched a man be killed on top of me.

Fimble had thrown the dagger, killing a member of his own pack. He gently picked me up from beneath my arms and helped me to my feet. He shook my body slightly to break my trance before handing me my stick. I dipped my head as I felt suddenly faint, forcing me to accept Fimble's hand as I steadied myself. My faintheartedness was an unwelcome trait from my mother.

He cupped my face before bringing his head closer to mine to grab my attention. "I will not hurt you. I will not let *anyone* hurt you. Right now, your castle is being ambushed. I need to get you away to safety," he said with authority. He used the same strong tone he had used with his sister when we had fought. I nodded my head vigorously, understanding his words.

We cautiously stuck our heads out from the library to evaluate who was close by. I heard Siesta somewhere nearby. Fimble tried to pull me away but I grabbed his arm, jarring him in my panic. "Wait," I said, pulling him toward where Siesta was. She heard my voice and hurried around the corner. Fimble and I were engaged in a silent struggle when she seen us, each pulling the other in a different direction.

"Lady Sia," she said with surprise. Her tone told me that she did not realize the danger we were in.

"Do you know where my parents are?" I demanded.

She jumped at my harsh tone, nodding "yes."

"You must go to them and tell them to escape. Inform everyone to run, we are being ambushed. Have someone ring the bell to raise the alarm."

"My lady?" she questioned, before registering the certainty in my eyes. She squared her shoulders and left in a determined manner. Fimble pulled me toward the front doors. I once again pulled him back.

"I cannot leave him," I said with Trim in mind. He knew at once who I meant. I turned and ran for the stairs, Ara at my heels before Fimble could respond. Fimble looked at the doors frantically before catching up with me. "We do not have time," he whispered harshly. Although his words opposed me, he was too good a wolf to leave someone behind. He then followed me wordlessly, seeing that I would not change my mind.

I came to the front of my door where Trim still slept. I slapped him hard on the face, hoping that he would wake. The herbs had worked far too well on him. The very thing I thought I was being clever at would now be my undoing. I tried lifting him but to no avail, his weight too heavy for my recovering body.

"If I carry him you will be defenseless. You are ill and I need to protect you," Fimble said, looking at me with his earnest eyes.

"I do not care about me! You must help me, Fimble. Please!" I begged, holding Lady Momiko's stick and moonstone close to my chest. "I will do my best to protect us, I promise. I can fight if I need to."

I could see my panicked words held little worth to him, but when he looked me in the eye, he could see my grim determination. He believed in me and my skills; he had said so already. Something not many people gave me credit for. The trust Fimble put in me to protect his life inspired me to believe my own words. *He believes in me and my fighting. He doesn't see me as fragile. He looks at me as an equal.*

I *would* protect us both.

He collected Trim and threw him over his shoulder before running down the stairs. I followed behind him, looking out for trouble. When we reached the wooden doors of the castle we came across one of Fimble's archers. He raised his bow to kill me but paused as he realized Fimble's alliance. Slowly he raised his weapon against us, taking aim.

I charged at him and used Lady Momiko's stick to swipe away his weapon. I barged him with my shoulder, knocking him toward the wall with all my might. We continued to run when he dropped to the ground. Screams erupted from inside the castle walls. Some of the huts had already been lit on fire and my pack fled from them, screaming.

I shouted out as I watched one of the wood choppers be stabbed to death by Lish. His gray ears pulled back when he heard my voice and he looked at us, narrowing his eyes on Fimble and me. The ringing of our bell echoed through the castle grounds, but we were too late.

"This way," Fimble said, running amongst the huts. He led me to Lady Momiko's hut. To my surprise he pulled aside the fur which hid my escape hole. *How does he know of this place?* "Go, go!" he said, pushing me along. I climbed into the hole and Ara followed. Fimble shoved Trim into the opening and I pulled him through, panting underneath the weight of his bulky body. Fimble quickly followed and together we stumbled through the tunnel, dragging Trim's lifeless body.

When we emerged from the other end of the tunnel, Fimble threw Trim over his shoulders and we ran together toward the trees. Ara and I lead the way. Two wolves that I did not recognize pursued us, their pace much quicker than our own. I dreaded having to defend us against two wolves at the same time. I hesitated to believe I could fight both of them if they caught up with us. Two arrows shot out from the trees and they both dropped to the ground, instantly dead.

I looked into the treetops as I ran, trying to determine the position of the archer. I was so frantic that I could not train my hearing on the wolf's location. A large black wolf suddenly dropped down into the shadows of the trees ahead. Her height was far greater than Fiesca's and her muscular frame was intimidating. When we caught up with her she said in a deep voice, "Let me take him, Fimble."

I stepped in front of Trim protectively, opposed to the idea of a foreign wolf carrying him. I assessed her as she looked back at me just as suspiciously. Her skin was shimmery black, with thick, short black hair and fur. She had great big canines which tipped over her lips and large orange eyes. Never had I seen a female wolf so large. I was mesmerized by her sheer size.

The wind carried the sound of screaming. Despair flooded my ears, forcing me back to the reality of my kingdom falling to ruins. The smell of smoke itched at my sensitive nose. I detected the horrific smell of burning flesh and fur. The screams echoed in my ears. My powerful hearing sent me into turmoil. I could not see their faces but their screams alone conveyed their fear and the undoing of my home and pack. I looked back at where the smoke began to stream into the sky. I feared for my parents. I swallowed my disgust at myself as I prepared to flee from my burning kingdom, my tail between my legs.

Chapter Sixteen- Surrealism

I found I was rooted to the spot. The screams echoed in my ears, disabling my legs. *I cannot move forward, I cannot run away from this.* I turned to see that Fimble had already begun to run alongside the woman who carried Trim, her strong legs unflinching under his weight. When Fimble's eyes met mine his face contorted with understanding. He knew I could not run from my loved ones when they were in danger. *I cannot abandon my own pack.*

I clutched at my ears, dropping to the ground as raised voices and screams penetrated my ears. Siesta's distant scream impaled my heart. As my panic began to mount I suddenly felt a warm mist descend upon me. I felt Lady Momiko's presence as if she were in front of me, smiling at me and covering me with a blanket. She was letting me know it would be all right.

I looked up at the smoke and destruction of my kingdom, then down to Lady Momiko's stick and moonstone, which no longer shined. My eyes widened as I thought of its meaning. *Does this mean Lady Momiko is...?* I closed my eyes at the thought.

"Sia, we can't, we must go," Fimble instructed, coming to my side.

"I cannot leave them!" I shouted at him through my tears. He looked helplessly at the other wolf, who then looked at me with a stern glare. I did not know who she was and yet I did not think of her as an enemy. "Can you protect him?" I asked, raising myself to my feet, ignoring Fimble.

"I do not take orders from you," she simply said. Her tone wasn't defiant or harsh, but it was clear that it was Fimble she obeyed and no one else.

"Rain, please," he said, his hands dangling by his side in defeat.

She looked between him and me with very little expression, but I sensed her compliance. "Thank you," I said, accepting her silence as agreement. "Ara, stay!" I shouted at her when she tried to run with me.

"Sia!" Fimble yelled out from behind me.

My body was still recovering but it felt stronger than it had only moments before. My strength and courage was building with each step. Although I was still not at my full strength, and I was unsure of what I could even do or whom I could save, I knew that cowering away from the safety of my pack was not something I could do.

Before long I had reached the tunnel and I squeezed into the small hidden hole in the castle wall easily. I made my way through the dark tunnel before breaking through to Lady Momiko's hut. I focused my hearing on Siesta's clumsy footing amongst the chaos. She ran through a hallway of the castle.

I made my way through the huts and searched through the billowing smoke. My heart was racing as I watched my fellow pack be hunted down before me. "Come here!" I said to the few cubs and young wolves that were in front of me. They had been ignored by the traitorous pack in favor of their parents. They were now alone, screaming and petrified, with nowhere to escape to. "Through there," I pointed to Lady Momiko's small passage.

One wolf came at them with a knife as they huddled together at the entrance of the hut. I appeared in front of him and grabbed his arm. I locked it and smashed my palm into his forearm, snapping it. The wolf screamed and I threw him into the ground, where he lay whimpering. I realized my own wildness and was distraught at how natural my violent actions had felt. During the scuffle the young wolves and cubs had made their escape and

I once again contemplated the flames, surveying the quickest route to the castle entrance.

I had trained all my life, but never had I before possessed the intent needed to harm other wolves so severely. And yet, the thrill of it swept over me. I once again recalled the murderous intent Phantom Wolves attempted to repress. *Is it because of this eye that I fight so well—and with no remorse for my actions?*

Another two wolves fell onto my path, blocking my view of the castle. Without hesitation I elbowed one in the stomach, knocking him back and swinging my arm around so I could punch the other one in the face. Her knife grazed my arm. I threw my stick up so that it flipped in the air. I caught it quickly and plunged the handle of it into her stomach. The male wolf came for me again. I wrapped my hand around the stick and swung it swiftly into the wolf's face as if it were an extension of my arm. I swung it behind my back, deterring the woman from ambushing me from behind while I determined if the male wolf would attack again. I turned quickly to her and lifted my leg high, kicking into her face. She fell to the ground and did not get back up. My feet grounded once again and I slightly wobbled, still not at my fullest strength— yet my reflexes were immaculate.

Siesta's scream echoed in my ears again, as if leading me to her. I could not see her but the echoes of her footsteps led me to believe she was running toward the bathing chambers. I ran toward her. I was unable to sense my mother or father; I could not collect their scent in the castle. *Please tell me they escaped*, I begged my Spirit Pack.

Running up the stairs I saw the flicker of a tail from a foreign wolf running through the hall toward Lady Momiko's room. I caught up with the wolf quickly and jumped on her back before she could open her door. I pulled on the woman's hair to force her to take steps back into the hallway again. She grabbed my arm and flung me into the wall. I gasped at the impact, my eyes widening in shock as she produced a knife that she had strapped to her thigh.

I rolled to my back and gathered into a protective crouch. My stick had been knocked away from my hands to Lady Momiko's door. She ran for me and just before she prepared to plunge the knife down on me, I used the strength of my legs to lift her, balancing her on my feet. Using all my core strength I flung her into the wall behind me. She smashed into a wall, releasing the knife. It dropped to the ground and I snatched it up from the ground and raised my arm to strike her with it. But as I did, she recoiled in fear, reminding me that she too was alive. I would be a murderer. Her eyes shone with fear. I paused as I battled my conflicting emotions. My hands shook with a desire to end her life, yet I knew that was not the true me who wanted to do such a thing.

She looked at me with terrified eyes as she huddled against the wall.

"Will you promise me that you will leave, that you won't hurt anyone?" I gasped, my voice shaky. I was irritated with myself for bartering with the attacking pack.

She looked at me with an astonished expression. "You will let me go?" she asked, surprised.

I glanced at her belly and hips that were covered in stretch marks. She had carried a cub in her belly. She was a mother and had a cub to return to; how could I take that cub's mother away?

"Return to your cub, but please do not hurt any more of my pack," I asked.

She held her stomach in disbelief, nodding her head vigorously at me in agreement. Although she came here to attack, the reality of it was that it was her Alpha, Kratin, who ordered this ambush; his pack must obey. My instinct told me that she would not harm anyone else and that this fight was not one that she

145

wanted to be a part of. I dropped the knife from my hand, unsure what I would have done had she continued to fight me. Perhaps I would have killed her. I was now relying on my instinct alone to evaluate how far she was a danger to my pack members. Was that the right decision?

She shakily stood up and began to back away from me. "Thank you, you are a fair and merciful wolf," she said, her voice scared. She scuffled away from me before fleeing down the hallway. I listened to her race down the stairs and past the library. I tracked her progress and noted that very quickly she had exited the castle grounds. I exhaled deeply, feeling that I had made the right decision.

I walked over to collect the stick from the ground, still clutching at Lady Momiko's moonstone. I carried it with me with every step that I took. I took a second to compose myself before I opened the door to her room, scared of what I would reveal.

Her door creaked open revealing a haven of peaceful quiet. It was as if sound did not penetrate the walls of the room. It was tranquil amongst all the chaos that surrounded it. The room was brightly lit by the sun, and in her bed, smiling, was Lady Momiko. Her hands were crossed over her chest and her eyes were closed as if she were sleeping. Her face was calm and open, though her old skin was paler than usual. I did not walk any further into the room; seeing her serene smile was enough for me. Lady Momiko had passed into her Spirit Pack. Amongst all the death and destruction she was smiling for our future. She had foreseen much, and although I did not yet know why she did certain things, I believed in her premonitions.

Siesta's scream reverberated through the hall, forcing me to recall what it was I had run up there for in the first place. I quietly closed Lady Momiko's door behind me before I ran to aid Siesta in the bathing chambers. I ran in and looked around frantically. My feet pulled up sharp as I witnessed Fiesca holding Siesta high in the air by the throat.

"Let her go!" I spat, unable to move from my position. Fiesca held her over the large opening in the wall. *We are two stories high, if she throws her...*

"I said, let her go!"

"Ah, Princess, you *are* still here," Fiesca smirked. Siesta grew blue in the face and I took a step forward. Fiesca shook her over the opening. "I wouldn't!"

"What do you want?" I demanded. My heart raced at she held Siesta hostage in front of me.

Fiesca's large brown eyes looked at me with disinterest. "Well, I am surprised that you are still here considering it was my brother's task to kill you," she remarked as her eyes locked on mine savagely. "Because you seem to have bewitched my brother, I would mostly say it is *you* I want."

"Then you can have me."

"No guard today, I see," she said, pretending to look over my shoulder. "Then it is you I will take." She threw Siesta away from her, into the open air. I screamed with my hand outstretched for hers. My vision blurred as I fell to my knees, crying aloud for Siesta. It felt as if time froze when I had just looked into Siesta's fear-filled eyes only seconds before her death, but my legs could not move fast enough. Time did not slow enough for me to save her. All I could do was watch as her body vanished into the air. I knew she had fallen to her death.

I screamed so loudly for her that I thought my lungs might erupt. My heart ruptured to lose one of my only friends. Her warm smile flashed into my mind, her soothing hands that swept through my hair, her calming voice. I thought of her excitement over her future, her wish for cubs, vanishing forever as she was thrown over. Fiesca stood back for a few seconds, enjoying my grief.

I wrapped my arms around me as I struggled for a breath. Fiesca quickly closed the distance between us and kneed me in the stomach. I hit the ground, the force of her attack dragging me along the floor. I flicked my head up, my hair flicking over. I growled savagely at Fiesca, my pain instantly turning into vicious hatred. I struggled to my feet, burning with anger.

We charged at each other simultaneously. She tried punching into me but I dodged her time and time again before punching into her stomach when she left herself open. I winded her and then elbowed her in the face. I swung my body around before jumping into her with force, kneeing her in the face.

She hit the ground and I stomped her face. Her blood splattered across the floor but I was not satisfied. I sat on her, punching into her face. She grabbed my arm before firmly flinging me over her shoulder. When she rolled over, I saw that her face was bloody.

She snarled at me, only furthering my invitation to attack her. I held Lady Momiko's moonstone firmly in my hand, drawing strength from it before I ran toward her again. She blocked my first punch, kneeing me in the jaw. I had to take a few steps back to regain my balance. She swung for me again and I swirled around her, using my small size and swiftness to my advantage. I grabbed her wrist and put all my might into pulling it back behind her back. She tried to spin round to catch a hold of me but when she did I twisted her wrist the other way, breaking it. She cried out in pain at the sudden snap. I kicked the back of her knee, dropping her in front of me. I wrapped my hands around her neck.

"Sia!" Fimble cried from behind me, panting heavily. My ear pulled back at his words, and my hands hesitated. No matter how badly they shook from a desire to snap her neck, I was hesitant to hurt Fimble. "Please, she is my sister."

"She killed Siesta," I said, the tears spilling over my left eye onto the top of Fiesca's long hair. Instead of using the strength I fathomed against Fiesca to kill her, I used it to maintain my hold on her.

"You are not like her, you are not a killer," he said, his own words confirming my own inner thoughts. *But she killed Siesta*, I thought to myself.

My hands dropped as I acknowledged that I couldn't do it. I couldn't kill her, no matter how much I wanted her dead. I could not do it with my own hands. I was once again pathetic.

"Leave, Fiesca," he said with savageness.

"You have truly turned against your own pack, for *her*?" she said with contempt.

I stood frozen. I was unsure if I could let her go. My hands still shook with murderous intent.

"I am guided by our mother's belief; she was kind-hearted, not like this bloodthirsty pack. I pity you for how far you have strayed from the values she taught us."

His words on morality reminded me of my own ethics. I pushed Fiesca away from me and she fell onto the floor. She scrambled to her feet without dignity. Fimble came to my side, pushing past her with his shoulder. He handed me Lady Momiko's stick without another word or glance to his sister. When I looked over his shoulder, I saw that she had already gone. "Sia, we must go."

I stared out from the opening of the wall, unwilling to move from the spot where I had last seen the friend I had lost. Fimble's warm hands curled over my shoulders, pulling me into him. He folded me into a comforting, friendly embrace. Together we turned from the bathing chambers and began to walk out.

My steps were slow, and I staggered on my feet. I looked at the blood that dripped from my hands and then to the hallway where I had let the other wolf escape. I slowed as I thought of Lady Momiko's peaceful slumber.

"Sia, we must run right now. Rain saw your parents escape from the back of the castle..." Fimble cupped my face, stroking his thumb over my closed eye that still shed tears for Siesta's death. "And so must you."

His words, touch, and mention of my parents brought me to my senses. I collected his hand in my own, grateful to have had him by my side. *I must live and not be fainthearted. I need to collect myself and be strong. I must return to Trim.*

Fimble stealthily led me back to Lady Momiko's hut. A few wolves attacked us but it was Fimble who fought them off. We ran across the open field toward where I had last left the others. I ran with Lady Momiko's stick and moonstone in one hand. My other hand clasped the moonstone Trim had given to me for my birthday. *My parents have escaped, at least they are safe.* I looked back over the thick smoke that engulfed my home. Suddenly a dark red liquid obscured my sight. I realized I was bleeding from my forehead. The surrealism of my own blood staining my one good eye compelled me to run faster. There were still wolves left who were worth fighting for. *I have to reach Trim and Ara to make sure they are safe.*

Chapter Seventeen- Foreseen

We ran past the beautiful watering hole that was usually so serene. I trained my sense of smell on the large wolf's scent— Fimble had addressed her as 'Rain.' Rain no longer ran into the distance; for some reason she was running back to greet us. I smelled a familiar scent running in front of her. Trim was awake and running back toward us. She was giving chase to him. He was closer than I first thought. My reflexes only gave me a brief warning of his proximity before the rustling of bushes stirred to my left. Trim jumped out of the bushes and pounced on Fimble.

They rolled over together across the grass before Trim gained the upper hand. Trim pinned Fimble on the ground but Fimble flipped him over his body. Trim pounced on him again, raising his claws to him. Rain caught his arm before he could use them as a weapon. Trim kicked into Rain's shin, knocking her grip from his hand. She wrapped her larger body around him in a stronghold. After a brief struggle he broke her hold over him and his eye fixated on Fimble again. Trim stopped himself from pouncing again when I stood in front of Fimble, who had already prepared himself for the fight. He was as surprised by my intervention as Trim.

"Don't!" I said with my hands outstretched in front of Fimble so Trim would not attack.

"What has happened to your face?" Trim demanded, although his words were not directed at me but at Fimble. "You attacked her!" Trim accused, while trying to sidestep me so he could reach him. Fimble continued dodging him. Trim's reflexes were much quicker than Fimble's. After all, Trim was one of the best warriors I had ever seen.

Rain once again pulled Trim off. He then began to fight her off as well.

My senses were assaulted by a multitude of scents—we were being chased. "Trim!" I screamed. I desperately tried to grab his attention, but he was in frenzy, fighting both Rain and Fimble. Ara barked at them viciously, trying to alert them to the danger. From afar I could see the others running amongst the trees. The small animals of the woods burrowed deep into the earth and hid amongst the branches of trees.

"Stop it!"

Finally they heard my words, but it was already too late. Ten wolves came for us. An arrow shot for me. Before I could jump out of its way, Trim had already jumped on me, rolling me onto the ground. He hunched over me protectively. His hand rested on my waist while he looked over my body quickly to make sure I had not been injured. When he was certain I had not been hurt, he raised himself from the ground and pushed me into the bushes to hide.

Rain attacked the two archers who shot arrows. She grabbed the bow from the first wolf and then sliced the string across his throat, wrapping it around. The effect was gruesome and I had to look away. She kicked the second wolf in the stomach, knocking him into the ground before she drove her claws deep into his chest. She looked up to find Fimble's location. He too was fighting the wolves and she quickly came to his side.

Fimble held a knife, gliding it elegantly over the wolves that attacked him. He sliced it over a wolf's chest and then over another's wrist as he attempted to use a long sword against him. After the wolf had fallen, Fimble collected the sword and used it as a second weapon. He and Rain fought off another two wolves with an easy grace, slicing through them as skillfully as the others. I watched them, awed at how well they worked together and how agile Fimble looked as he fought. It was as if they were locked in a ghastly dance as they moved together as one to slay their attackers.

Trim snapped the neck of another of the wolves before grabbing the body and throwing it toward another oncoming attacker. The wolf tried to throw the body's weight off him but Trim was already on him, savagely cutting his claws across the wolf's throat. He grabbed the knife his victim had used as a weapon and looked around for his next target.

One of the wolves tried to run past him to get to me. Trim stabbed the knife into his stomach, pulling it out and slitting his ankles so he fell instantly. He threw the knife at the remaining wolf that tried to retreat—the last of those who had attacked us. The knife was like a dagger straight to the back of the neck and the wolf instantly dropped.

I held Ara tightly, shielding her from all those who had attacked us. When Trim was satisfied we were no longer in danger he came to where I was partially hidden in the bushes and crouched beside me. "Have you been hurt?" he asked, taking my hand and slowly pulling me out of the bushes. I shook my head at him immediately so he knew I was not injured. He raised his hand to my forehead, assessing the injury I had acquired when I fought in the castle.

I felt embarrassed and weak for listening to Trim and hiding in the bushes like a coward. Despite the fact that I was well-trained and competent in a fight, I shied away from conflict. *Does this make me a failure as a warrior?* Perhaps this is why everyone saw me like this: weak, fragile and always in need of protection.

"Sia, my dear, are you all right? You are unharmed, yes?" Fimble asked worriedly as he paced over to my side.

"It is not of your concern," Trim declared as he shielded me from Fimble's sight.

"It is my concern if I permit it to be. I do not fear you, nor do I really care about what happens to you. But not only will I protect her, I will also give her the option to participate in the fight if that's what she wants. I won't simply push her aside," Fimble challenged.

"You know nothing about us and you have no right to her," Trim replied coldly.

I cowered from their harsh tones. I was unsettled that they should disagree over me. They only differed about my protection. But my heart was lifted by Fimble's words. Perhaps he did see me as a brave fighter, a warrior. It felt good to be acknowledged for my capabilities, but I did not feel I could deny Trim his protectiveness over me either.

"I know already what I need to. And when it comes to Sia I have already firmly made up my mind," Fimble said sharply. I didn't understand the intention behind those words. But because of them, Trim visibly stiffened, his clenched fists shaking noticeably by his side. "We need to leave now," Fimble announced, picking up the two bows and arrows.

I grabbed Trim's hand before he could attack Fimble yet again. Trim was usually so blank and impassive that I could not read his emotions. But now he boiled over to the extent that I could see the muscles tightening beneath his skin. He wanted to fight Fimble. What had shaken him so badly? Perhaps the traumatic events of the last few days were enough to penetrate through his hard exterior—it certainly seemed as though he had reached breaking point.

"Fimble helped us escape the castle," I said, defending him so Trim would hold back. I needed him to hear me out. Fimble had endangered his own life at my request. He had carried Trim to safety, leaving himself vulnerable to attack.

"His pack has just ambushed our home, and on top of that, he let you go back," Trim countered. His expression was not as concealed as it usually was. He was clearly upset as he looked down at my bloodied hands.

"I am not of that pack anymore, no matter how you look at it. They will soon hunt me as well. I am now a traitor to them," Fimble said as he eyed the corpses that littered the ground around us. "I will tell you everything I know, but for now, we must get away from here. Even if you do not have faith in my words, you must realize it is safer for us all if we travel together."

Trim did not reply. They stared at each other, sizing each other up. I still held onto Trim's hand, unsure how he would act. I was worried he would unsheathe the knife strapped to his chest. If Trim still misunderstood then I did not doubt he would kill Fimble. But I did not want that. Even now, I doubted whether I was making the right decisions and I couldn't narrow my thoughts on one decisive action. My mind tugged in so many directions.

"I think," I said quietly, grabbing Trim's attention, "I want to go with them, and hear what Fimble has to say. I want to know why they have done this."

Trim's eye narrowed on my hidden green eye that was still heavily bandaged. A shudder ran through me as I felt it was not me he was really seeing but the ghost of his mentor. I clutched Lady Momiko's stick and moonstone to my chest under his intense glare. Slowly I released my hold of him, allowing him to think for himself, instead of only about my needs.

"I will protect you, Sia," Fimble promised with confidence.

"It is not you who needs to worry about protecting her," Trim shot back savagely. I felt sorry for what I done to Trim. It must have been so disorientating for him, waking up from his drugged state to this madness. I had denied him the chance to protect his home, to protect our pack. If I had not sabotaged his drink then I doubted so much of this would've happened. I would definitely be safe, Siesta would still be alive, my parents and most of my pack would be with me. Trim probably hated me right now for taking his rights away from him. I hated myself for doing it.

I walked beside Fimble, stricken with my grief and shame. I did not want to walk alongside Trim in case he admitted out loud my mistake. By putting Trim to sleep, I had left our home utterly defenseless. I had made a severe mistake but I could not yet face the words of blame; they already rested so heavily on my shoulders. In a way I felt as if I was hiding behind Fimble. Right now I couldn't handle Trim's reproaches.

"We will find a place of rest and then talk, Sia," Fimble said earnestly. He paused for me to catch up with him before grabbing my shoulders and pulling me into him. He rubbed my back to help warm me up. I did believe in Fimble's words and I felt protected by him. I wanted to find out more about what had happened. But for now I only wanted to be held. My shoulders slumped when I thought about all I had lost.

Trim followed shortly behind. Our fast pace soon turned into a run that continued for half a day. I don't know how I gathered the strength to do it, but I would not allow myself to let anyone down. I did not want to be the weakest link that jeopardized them all.

Rain was always ahead of us, her speed unmatched because of her long, muscular legs. She kept a look out in front of us. When it turned dark and the moon glowed above us we finally decided to make camp. Thankfully it was a warm night because we couldn't create fire in case it drew attention to our position.

I sat against a tree with Ara curled in my lap, stroking through her fur with my bloodied hands. Rain had gone to find water and Trim stood close by on watch. Fimble sat beside me, looking at Ara as I stroked her. "What has happened to your eye?" he asked. I felt Trim's eye on me instantly, intimidating me from telling him the truth. I shifted uncomfortably under the question. I felt I could trust Fimble and yet, because of Trim and my parents' words of caution, I could not say.

"I caught a bug in my eye, it infected it immensely," I said my voice shaky under the obvious lie.

Fimble gave me a small crooked smile; he knew my words were not truthful. "You may not feel it is safe to tell me now, but soon you will come to trust me." He looked up at the moon. "But for now, I hope your eye gets better."

"Are you not going to tell us what you know so we can leave?" Trim intervened harshly, now standing in front of us. I shuffled slightly away from Fimble under Trim's stern look.

Fimble exchanged an irritated look with him. "The ending of your story about the Phantom Wolf was not accurate. There was one who made it out alive," Fimble admitted hesitantly.

Trim's face was still stern but I could see the glimmer of hope wash through his eye before he quickly concealed his emotion. He hoped that Sia, the Phantom Wolf, was still alive. But I had seen her death.

Fimble turned to me, "Sia... your uncle, Taleb, is still alive."

"That's not possible," Trim rejected. "Sia killed him just before her human, Thomas."

"Not entirely correct. She ripped off his left ear and ripped into his throat, yet he is still alive. You see for the last few years he has been visiting my father. Everyone knows who Taleb is, and his black fur is evidence enough that he is of the royal pack. Normally my father would not cater for such an arrogant wolf, but Taleb used our fear of humans as a tool to engage with our pack.

He claimed he wanted to take back kingship... that his brother, Saith, and his queen, Keeley, were short-sighted about the true threat of the humans that lingered not that far from us. He claims he can control the humans and he has many other packs who believe this. They are so frightened of the humans that they have conspired with him to take back the kingdom."

I looked over at Trim worriedly. I saw that his thoughts mirrored my own. How were we so blind to this? Was this what Lady Momiko predicted would happen? If she saw it then why would she lead the very same pack directly into our home? We had to trust that there would have been a far worse outcome if we hadn't chosen this path.

"Unfortunately he also gained the trust of my father, but I could see him for who he was and what he truly wanted. After years of recovering from his severe injuries that he suffered at the hands of the Phantom Wolf, he began to build an army of followers. I don't know where it is they are based, but it was my pack he wanted to use for his first attempt in ambushing the castle. Lady Momiko's foresight was our focus. We were to come and kill her so you would have no knowledge of his plan and therefore remain vulnerable. He also wanted us to kill Saith and Keeley. It was quite the coincidence and surprise when we were invited for your birthday celebrations. He implied that he had planned everything. However, I feared that it was not he who had organized our meeting. I thought that perhaps Lady Momiko had already seen our plans. He has somehow managed to look like a far greater wolf than he really is."

I thought of the dream I had where someone had snuck into Lady Momiko's room and stabbed her to death. I wondered if it were the very same thing she had seen. But why would such a thing be presented to me in my dreams? My mind raced. Perhaps she had initiated the meeting then hid until she knew her time was up—when they would trigger their ambush.

"What made *you* change your mind? Why didn't you attack me?" I asked thinking of the prime opportunity he had to kill me.

"Lady Momiko," he said simply. "The original plan was for us to find her first and kill her in case she had seen anything and warned you. We searched for her for many nights but to no avail, we could not find her.

I was walking through the woods only yesterday afternoon, and she was waiting for me. It seemed she knew everything. Taleb thought he had control of it, the reality was he did not—she did," he smiled. "She was not threatened by me and made it very clear she knew why I came. She already knew who I was. She used certain things against me, one might say: my mother's kindness; my instinctual feeling that Taleb was lying; that my pack had been fooled; that I didn't want blood on my hands; and you," he gestured toward me.

"So Lady Momiko convinced you," Trim simply said with his arms crossed over his chest.

"To put it simply, yes. Rain was close by as she always is. She already knew of my private opinions concerning our mission. When I decided I didn't want to fight alongside my pack, well, she was here as a precaution. I tried to do as my father wished, but when it came down to it and I held that knife in my hand to kill you, Sia, I just couldn't. Lady Momiko's words, they were true and wise. She had already seen it all, and she knew I would drop that blade and choose to protect you against Taleb. Such a wolf, Taleb, should not exist."

Wherever my parents currently were in hiding, I prayed to my Spirit Pack that they already knew who it was that orchestrated the attack on our home.

"What do we do now?" I asked Trim. "If Taleb is still alive, and our pack is now scattered, then how do we fight against them?"

"Actually," Fimble interjected, "Lady Momiko said that we were to look to you, that soon you will know how."

My mouth widened but I said nothing. A small gust of cool wind swept past us and I shivered. Rain appeared with water in a canteen. I accepted some from her, grateful for the opportunity to divert their intense eyes from me.

"How far is the watering hole from here?" Trim asked Rain.

"Only of a few minutes' walk south of here," she replied, offering Fimble the canteen.

Fimble drank some water and then offered his hand to me, reminding me of my bloodstained hands. "Sia, we shall go clean you up, we cannot very well have you looking like this when you are reunited with your parents."

I took his hand, still holding Lady Momiko's stick and moonstone in the other. I clung to them like they were my only answer. If she had foreseen all of this, then she would have given me these gifts for a purpose. But why had she, before her death, kept so much hidden from us?

And if this Phantom Wolf eye—my curse—was not her third gift, then what was?

Chapter Eighteen- Learning to let go

$\mathcal{T}$rim and I walked in silence to the water as we let the situation sink in. As we both privately reflected over the new information, I couldn't help but feel that the news of Taleb's survival affected Trim more so than me. His death was the reason why the Phantom Wolf, Sia, had taken her own life, so Taleb could no longer do sinful things, especially after he turned her lover, Uncle Kiba, into a Phantom Wolf.

Taleb somehow controlled that human Thomas who had killed her and cursed her. Now to find out that Taleb was still alive was terrifying, especially as he was announcing to other packs that he could control the humans. I knew that the very mention of the humans struck fear into the heart of wolves, causing our kind to separate in their panic. But no one had witnessed a human since the days of Thomas—well, until I had seen those two humans. My heart raced as I contemplated the coincidence of finding humans roaming around our land. I could only speculate about whether or not Taleb knew of their existence.

Surrounding us was a dense forest and only a small amount of the moon's light broke through the leaves. We found the secluded spot just where Rain described it. The watering hole was small but it looked deep. Noises from the animals echoed through the trees, jolting my already frayed nerves. I couldn't help but punish myself with the ironic thought that I had always wanted to be wild in nature—to be free from the restraints attached to my royal position. It seemed I had gotten my wish, but the circumstances that had allowed it were horrifying. The cruel reality of my new situation dispelled all the pleasure of being in nature.

"Sia?" Trim called, already partly submerged in the water. A sliver of moonlight highlighted his chiseled jaw and the glistening water on his chest. He held his hand out to me. "We need to get you clean. We should also wash the dressing of your bandage."

I looked around warily, checking that Fimble or Rain hadn't followed us to the watering hole. Although they were still close, the distance we had put between us was sufficient to hide my Phantom Wolf eye. I looked at Ara. She didn't seem unsettled, which was confirmation enough for me that we were alone. I placed Lady Momiko's belongings on the ground and walked into the cold water, shivering as I remembered the luxury of hot water I had recently enjoyed each night. I waded over to him through the water where he waited for me. Ara sat patiently by the water edge, eyeing the animals of the forest. I unraveled my bandage and looked through my Phantom Wolf eye. Once again everything was brighter. It was as if it were daytime for my right eye, but night for my left.

"Does it hurt you?" he asked, taking the bandage out of my hand. It was filthy and had absorbed a small amount of blood from the scratch on my forehead. I shivered as I remembered my dream only nights before, recalling a time of innocence when I had asked him the very same question.

"Not right now, but everything is brighter. I can see more," I said honestly. During the night the vision of my eye compensated for the effect it had on me during the day. In the daytime the Phantom Wolf eye could not handle the piercing bright light of the sun because of its severe sensitivity and heightened sight. But at night, when so dark, my vision was normal. Night became day. In time I hoped I would adjust to its affects by learning to control it.

"Everything of a Phantom Wolf is enhanced: your speed, stamina, balance, fighting skills. You can see much more..." Trim trailed off as he scrubbed my bandage and then flicked it out.

"When I went back to the castle, it scared me," I said, grabbing his attention. "I wanted to hurt wolves so badly that I almost killed two. It came as a reflex, but I don't want to be like that. But because I didn't kill them I felt as though I had failed my pack... that I couldn't protect them. It would've been so easy to kill them both, and yet I forfeited my desire. Do you think I have failed my pack?"

"I believe that just because you choose not to take another wolf's life does not mean you are weak. That is my job, not yours. I bitterly regret not being there to protect you," he said, reaching his hand out to my forehead. He wiped at the dry blood and assessed my wound for a moment. "It has already healed."

"What? But that is not possible," I questioned, looking into my own reflection in the still water and wiping at the cut. It had already completely healed.

"Phantom Wolves can also heal very quickly, but Sia, you must consider their specific dietary requirements as well." He washed water over himself, wiping the dirt from his hard chest and muscular arms.

"Dietary?" I repeated, mesmerized. I couldn't look away as he washed over his masculine frame. I fell victim, like I always did, to my desire for him. It seemed I was always an on-looker; I could never touch.

"Phantom Wolves live in a state of both death and life. When Sia lived she could only eat freshly killed animals. That is a trait you too have acquired. I sniffed your bowl the day when you thought your meat had been sitting for too long, it was fine. It was just your body reacting to it; your Phantom Wolf eye must have already been in transition."

He had sniffed my meal, and he didn't react as if it were bad. When ill I had asked him if there was something wrong with my meat, and he had answered honestly that there was not. Did my parents know I was reacting to the meat in such a way because of my eye?

"Why do you think she cursed me with this eye?" I asked Trim.

He stopped washing over himself and looked at me directly before looking up to the moon. He ran his fingers through his hair as he fought to find the right words to honor her memory. "She was kind, no matter how many people believed her otherwise. I knew her well. I think for whatever reason she has given it to you to aid you in some way. No one knew of the hatred for Phantom Wolves more than her—she even despised herself for being such a creature. But I believe if she has done this to you, then she has done so for a good reason," Trim said quietly.

My heart pained at how lovingly he spoke of her. He looked up to her in so many ways. I felt foolish for ever thinking it possible I could provoke the same level of affection from him. I washed over my arm and found another wound that had almost healed. I washed through my hair because it felt filthy and smelled of smoke. I dunked my head under the cold water, wanting to stay there forever.   I curled into a small ball beneath the water, pretending as if time had stopped. A migraine ruptured in my head, forcing me to break the surface of the water, spluttering hysterically.

"Sia?" Trim panicked.

I coughed uncontrollably while crawling to the edge of the water. I felt as though I had swallowed too much water and could not breathe. But it wasn't that. I could still see my surroundings: the bushes, trees, Ara who barked in my face. Trim shook me vigorously and I used his large arms for support, trying to hold myself up. I was in a state of consciousness, still coherent to what was happening around me, yet simultaneously I felt as though I were elsewhere. Suddenly I was unable to move. My body froze and it seemed as though I was being channeled for something.

My vision faded in and out, focusing on a different place—a small cave with a fire. Then I would again return to the watering hole. Reality vanished once again and my sight was then upon the image of the cave. Slowly it focused in as if I were walking toward it myself. I looked into the cave and saw the same humans I had run into only days before.

The male was wrapped around his kin for warmth. They shook in the cold. The vision I was being shown narrowed in on the little girl's shin that was now infected. As if the human had physically seen me he gathered a piece of wood and gestured for me to get away from them.

My mind was pulled back to my physical body through a path that I tried to memorize. The vision led me through trees and along a graveled trail. Vivid green foliage surrounded me as though I were in a forest. I could hear the noises of a thousand small animals that hunted for their food. The path blurred into streaks of green because of the speed with which the vision swept me back. The path connected me to them from where I stood now.

I gasped as I was flung back into myself. I took what felt like my first breath in a long time. My small claws firmly dug into Trim's arm. I came to understand the reality of the situation. Did I just have a vision?

"Sia, what is wrong?" Trim gasped.

I loosened my grip on him, which had caused him to lightly bleed. How hard was I grasping onto him? Never had I had such an outer body experience. I stroked my hand through my thick hair shakily, trying to distract myself and gather my thoughts.

"The humans, I saw the humans," I thought out loud, still trying to make sense of it. Lady Momiko was the only one I knew who could see things. I thought of her last dying words to me. She had asked me what I would do with such a gift. I burrowed my eyebrows in confusion. My hand grabbed a clump of the dirt so I could try and focus on the place I was now. The pull I felt to the cave was immense. There was no way I could be mistaken. "It was a premonition," I revealed to Trim.

His face eased at once. If Trim did not panic, then I knew everything would be okay. "A premonition like Lady Momiko used to have?"

"I believe so," I said, trying to stand up. I was exhausted. Trim picked up Lady Momiko's stick and moonstone for me.

"Use this for support when you walk." He offered the walking stick to me. "Often when Lady Momiko saw things it would weaken her body significantly. What were you shown?"

"Trim," I said holding my breath as the seriousness of my tone grabbed his attention. I had forgotten that it was only me who knew Lady Momiko had now passed over to the spirit world. "When I returned to the castle and went to Lady Momiko's room... she had passed."

The heavy air swept around us, and his features remained as expressionless as always. I knew he was upset, I could feel him breaking, but he did not convey that pain on his face. "I see," he simply said, looking away from me. "What was it you saw in your premonition?"

He had dismissed the conversation. He covered even the pain of Lady Momiko's death with his hard, expressionless exterior. But if this was his way of dealing with it, I could not push any further on the matter. "It was a cave," I pointed into its direction, as certain as if I had been there. Well, in a way, I had. I knew how to track the humans from here because of the path I was shown. "The humans were there... the little one, she is injured."

"Then we need to go kill them," Trim snapped.

"We cannot!" I shouted. I was taken aback by my own passion. "I can't explain the feeling I have but I know that we must protect them."

"Sia, are you crazy? If Taleb finds them then we are all as good as dead. On top of that they are *humans*. They have no place in this world."

"I cannot just ignore what I feel," I said with my hand on my chest. "I know I have been shown this image to help them. I can't explain the feeling, but I just... *know*."

"That's the problem, Sia, you think you always know what is best." He looked away when he realized what he had said. In other circumstances speaking to royalty like that would have been inappropriate.

I gathered my strength upon Lady Momiko's walking stick, using it to stand tall. "I know I have done many foolish things in the past, but do you honestly think that I would lie in such a situation?" I said, hurt by his words. He still mocked me, treated me like a cub.

"I promised your parents, and you, from a young age I would protect you. Around humans is not somewhere I can do that," he said, his voice shaky. He drew himself up from his crouched position so that we stood facing each other.

"I want to ask you to make me one promise," I said heavily. "I am not that cub anymore, and I stand in front of you as a woman. So promise me now, you will protect me how I am or I give you my consent to no longer follow me. But, either way, I will be going there."

He looked back at me steadily from his blue eye. Our intimate stare lingered as the wind brushed through us, rustling the leaves around us. His face was so close to mine. I had to hold my own body back, as I could barely resist the urge to feel his lips on mine. The stress of the situation only made me feel more desperate for his touch. Trim's lips parted and his hand reached for my cheek. The look he gave me was so raw that I was sure he too felt the same desire.

His hand paused before he even touched me. I sucked my breath in, my eyes pleading with him to continue. But he closed his fist and looked away. My eyes dropped to the ground as I exhaled. The fierce pull we had toward each other shattered instantly in front of me, leaving me cold. I was so convinced he too wanted such a thing. I stood there shocked for a long moment before I could breathe once again. I forced myself to turn and walk away.

"Sia," Trim's voice was stern once again, "...your bandage."

I grabbed it out of his hand, seeing it as more than just an object. It was concealing my identity, concealing a lie. *Lies—what I hate most.* Exactly what I was forced to do in front of everyone I met. But it could not be helped; I knew the repercussions involved if others knew of this eye. I heard of the stories about previous Phantom Wolves and how they were hunted. Everyone feared them because they were connected with a human. They were monsters and everyone wanted them dead. I did not want others to tremble at my appearance. I did not want to have those whom I trusted and believed in to turn on me.

I had my first premonition. *Was it only this once, perhaps guidance from my Spirit Pack? Or was it Lady Momiko's third gift?* After all, she had asked me what I would do with such an ability, and back then I could not give her an answer. *I still can't.*

I wrapped the bandage around my eye, covering it. I began to walk toward where Fimble and Rain rested.

"We cannot stay with them forever. I do not trust him," Trim called out from behind me. I turned to see his hands held in the air in a gesture of annoyance.

"Is it that you do not trust him, or that you do not trust him around me?" I asked arrogantly. It was very obvious Trim had no designs on me as a woman so I did not know why it rattled him when Fimble spoke so fondly of me. I was confused because in certain heated moments, I felt as if it were not only me that was enticed, but Trim as well—that he wanted the same thing as me and that was our togetherness.

But perhaps I was only deluded by my first love. The feelings I thought we shared may have been an illusion. He did not trust Fimble and now I found myself using that against him. I wanted to get a reaction from him like Fimble could so easily. I wanted to read his expression and know what he was thinking, and so, I used "Fimble" and "me" in the same sentence. It had certainly irritated Trim before.

His hands dropped to his sides, but he did not speak. I turned from him and clutched at Lady Momiko's stick, forcing myself to walk away from him. Whenever I looked at him I was hopeful, but his impassiveness led me to see the truth. *I must learn to let him go.*

Chapter Nineteen- Lifeless Body

Trim walked several paces behind me while Ara kept by my side. In the distance I could see Fimble and Rain speaking to one another intently. When she heard me approach, Rain looked up at me, her deep voice quietening into a secretive whisper.

I wanted to protect the humans; the pull over me was far too great to deny. I could not yet trust Trim on this matter, but Fimble I knew believed in me. I could rely on his honesty. If he didn't want a part in pursuing the humans then so be it, but if he did then I knew it would be without an ulterior motive.

"You said I could trust you, didn't you?" I asked Fimble. I had already made my decision.

"Yes, with anything, Sia," Fimble said, stepping toward me.

When he spoke so earnestly I knew I could follow my instinct. He had shown me I could trust him and I did not think him capable of deception. "What do you think of humans?" I asked directly, monitoring both his and Rain's reactions.

"That some regard them as a mere myth, but I believe they must exist for such stories to be told," Fimble replied, slightly confused by the direction the conversation had taken.

"If I lead you to two humans whose whereabouts I know of, would you execute them on the spot? Or because I ask this of you now, would you offer them protection?" I asked boldly, watching Rain's response. Much like Trim, she did not show her thoughts on her face.

"I am sorry, she is deranged after today's events," Trim broke into our conversation.

"I am not deranged," I said to Fimble, overlooking Trim, who had raised his hand to my mouth to silence me.

"Are you trying to get us killed?" he savagely whispered. I lightly bit his hand, but hard enough so that he would retract it.

"Fimble, I need your word. I think I have been gifted with Lady Momiko's sight, and this is what I have been shown," I explained, pushing aside Trim. If Trim would not follow me then that was his choice, but I would not reject such a strong message or my instinctual knowledge.

"Are you certain you have her sight?" Fimble asked, intrigued. "Is that the reason for your covered eye?"

Trim let out a sign of irritation before shooting me a reproving look. The shadows of the trees cloaked his scar and only his bright blue eye was visible. I wanted to tell Fimble the truth more than ever, but Trim's harsh glare pulled me back. I wanted to reveal my Phantom Wolf eye but I remembered the caution in my parents' words.

"You will either follow me or go your own way—I don't mind which—but that is my intended direction," I stated strongly. Whether they wanted to follow in the same direction as me or not, I intended to find the humans. I would appreciate their company, but if they could not support me then our journey ended here, and I would probably not see either of them again. Trim breathed out in relief that I had not mentioned my Phantom Wolf eye.

Fimble exchanged a look with Rain before deciding their fates. "We will go with you, but why do you want to protect the humans, Sia? You know what they are capable of."

"I know, and so did Lady Momiko, and so did my Spirit Pack, and yet it is what I have been shown. I cannot explain the sensation but I know that is what I must do," I explained impatiently.

"You cannot do anything in such a state," Rain interjected, her tone firm. "You must rest for the night and then upon daybreak we will travel to this destination. But Fimble also needs rest. I will watch over us through the night. You especially, little Princess, need rest, or you will be our weakness."

"I agree," I said, before either Fimble or Trim could argue. Usually I would have been offended but I had learned much about myself in the past few days. I was a half-formed version of what I thought I was: free, wild, a fierce fighter. After so many traumas, I was too weak to face the situation head-on. I could not protect myself in this condition. I could not kill, and I *did* need Trim to guard me. "I will not let anyone down."

*

As pretty as our words were about needing rest for strength, we were all too affected by the day's events to properly sleep. Fimble and I were the only ones who even attempted it, while Rain and Trim stayed awake watching over us all night.

The respite the night afforded was enough for my body to recover. I could feel the difference that the Phantom Wolf eye played on my body. It allowed me to heal quickly, countering the effect the vision had had on my body. Eventually I went to sit on a nearby rock that was in plain sight of the others. I fixated on Lady Momiko's words while rolling the moonstone in my hand. They were far enough away that I could call her name under my breath without their hearing. Lady Momiko had said that even after her death I could use the stone to call upon her. I whispered her name into the darkness, and I constantly thought about her, but I could not seem to summon her. I felt dim-witted as I tried to call her forth from the darkness.

"They will not come unless it is a full moon," Rain said quietly, walking over to me. It would be a few hours until the sun rose. Fimble still tried his hardest to rest, although he was tossing and turning relentlessly. Trim watched over us broodily as he ate an apple. I could tell he was listening in on our conversation as his orange ears perked up. Rain looked at him and then evidently disregarded him, unconcerned if he had heard. "Your Spirit Pack?"

"How do you know that?" I asked, hiding the stone beneath me.

"One might say I have a lot of time on my own to acquire information on many things," she said, her deep voice smooth and soothing.

"How did you and Fimble meet? Is he your desired mate?" I asked intrusively. I saw how she looked at him.

"I am not such a wolf he could see in that way. But it does not matter how we are together. I will stay close to him to protect him, just as he did for me a long time ago," she said as she watched him sleep. "When I was little, I was abandoned by my pack because of my larger size... they thought I had a deformity. I was close to death when he found me. He looked after me, brought me a bow and arrow so I could learn to hunt on my own. He gave me some lessons when he could sneak away from his pack. I was so fixated on impressing him back then that I surpassed him at archery within months."

I looked at the bow and arrow on her back. It suited her strong frame. I could not imagine anyone exceeding Fimble's archery skills. She laughed lightly at my incredulous expression.

"He now practices regularly to surpass *me*," she said, gesturing toward her bow. She lined three arrows on her bow at once. She closed one eye in concentration, just as he did, and took aim. I was doubtful that she could simultaneously shoot three. Her strong hand let go of the string, and the three arrows shot into the tree in a perfect line.

"Why are you showing this to me?" I asked in awe. I did not want her to feel that she had to prove her skills.

"Because I will follow Fimble until my death, and if it is you that he desires to follow and protect right now, then I must prove my skills and worth to you also. I will protect you if he cannot." Her orange eyes moved over to Fimble in adoration.

"There is no need to protect me. I can see you do not trust me," I said honestly, catching her smile as I said it.

"I will protect you if Fimble says I am to, but I will turn on you just as quickly if he were to command it. That would be a fight I would look forward to," she said, nodding toward Trim. "I don't trust you. I don't like what is hidden behind your bandage because if you must hide it, then it is something that you are concealing from Fimble... something that could alter the circumstances in some way."

"An interesting idea," I said casually, pushing my irritation down. I could not be insulted by the words she spoke. It was the truth. Everything she said was only in the best interests of Fimble.

"But I can see how he looks at you, so for now, Princess, I will look out for you, but I do advise you to reconsider your foolish notion about protecting humans." The wind caught her short wiry hair, fanning it across her face.

"Both you and Fimble are free to choose what path you desire most, but within a few short hours I will be walking toward the humans and I will protect them when I find them. If you do not share my intentions then you should not come," I said, standing and walking over to Trim. The conversation exhausted me. I understood her caution on all the things she voiced concern over, but I did not need more doubt placed into my mind.

"You should eat this," Trim said, offering me a rabbit that had been freshly killed. It was a rabbit with the same black fur as my own. I looked at it, pained to think of my mouth biting into such fresh meat, my teeth connecting with its fur and ripping into the moistness of its flesh. My stomach curled at the thought.

"I cannot," I said, not in defiance, but with simple realization. My love for animals stopped me from eating animals directly, or even raw slabs of meat. The thought alone made me sick. The vision was too repulsive to turn into reality. Trim raised it closer to my face so that the fresh blood caught my nose. I tried to will myself to accept it, knowing I had to restore my energy.

I fed it to Ara, who was more than happy to receive such a treat.

"Sia," he said in an irritated tone, as if I were being ungrateful.

"I cannot do it," I said angrily. "I will find another way." No matter how hungry I was and how much I wanted to eat it, I could not bring myself to rip into its lifeless body. I physically could not put the creature's body to my mouth. "I just can't."

Chapter Twenty- Revelation

My memory of the cave's location was phenomenal. There was no indecision in my steps; I knew exactly where I was walking. We were cautious, however, knowing that at any time one of our pursuers could be close.

We did not speak as I was too focused on my mission. I simply stared ahead instead of starting conversation with the others that followed behind. I was determined to be proven right about where the humans were hiding. At least then I would no longer doubt myself.

We edged closer to the location I had prophesied. I raised my hands to the others to indicate to them to stop walking. I sniffed and caught the faint scent of the male I had previously made contact with. *So, they are here.*

"Stay here," I commanded, still walking with Lady Momiko's stick. I did not need it to walk but I had grown accustomed to the slight tinkling of the bells as they swayed with my movement. Her moonstone I held firmly in my hand, resting it on the handle of the stick.

I walked forward and noted with annoyance that none of them stayed back, even after I had specifically requested it. The cave came into sight. Ara was the closest to me and I watched as she lowered her nose to the ground and tensed. I looked through the shadows of the trees to where I could smell the human. How had no one else found them? I looked at our surroundings, judging that the cave was in a secluded location. The minerals of the cave walls somewhat dampened their already faint scent. If I had not known they were here specifically, I would not have found them. I questioned if it were a calculated move on their part or merely a happy coincidence. Either way, it had certainly paid off for their safety.

I dipped my head and crouched lower in the bush in which I was hiding as I watched the male human come out. He was wearing the same odd material he had on his body when we had first met. The material was ragged and stained with filth. He walked out with a small cylinder container before looking both ways to make sure no one was around. He turned the cylinder upside down and a small droplet of water dropped onto the dirt. *Was this how humans carried their water?*

I stepped out from the bushes, no longer able to hide. Curiosity drove my steps forward and I approached him tentatively. The rustling of the bushes created only a faint sound but enough to arouse his panic. He picked up a nearby stick— much like my vision had shown me he would, though the circumstances were slightly different. The vision had shown them resting next to a flame at night. That must have been why the stick he had prodded me with in my vision had flames on it.

"Stay away!" he demanded. His mousy brown hair was oily and scruffy and I could not help but stare at him. He shouted so confidently for me to stay back but his legs trembled at the sight of me.

"You remember me," I said soothingly. I took a hesitant step toward him. The human threatened me with the stick and Trim did nothing to help the delicate situation when he stepped aggressively out of the bushes.

"I remember you!" the male yelled, pointing the stick firstly at Trim and then at Fimble and Rain who walked out behind him.

"It is true," Fimble said, his voice distant, "humans exist!"

"Stay inside, Reina!" the human yelled at the young girl who had come out of the cave. Her expression was curious, probably about why her brother was yelling. My eyes were instantly drawn to her shin, which was obviously infected.

"We are not here to hurt you," I said calmly, indicating for him to lower his stick.

"He is a threat to us," Trim loudly interrupted.

At such a sensitive time it was not appropriate for him to speak so openly. It only made the human more anxious. "Now is not the time to say such things out loud, Trim," I responded angrily. "You are no help to the situation, especially since it was you who last attacked him."

"Because they are *human,*" he simply said. His face flushed at my sudden outburst. "It is in our very nature. I cannot dismiss the warning we have grown up with simply because you want me to."

"I did not force you to come," I replied angrily. I closed my eyes in frustration at our sudden immature argument.

Ara approached the cave, sniffing in the direction of the girl. The human male automatically held the stick out toward her in an aggressive manner. A growl ripped out of my mouth, warning him to not hurt her. Ara simply continued forward nonchalantly.

"I am serious!" he yelled, swiping at Ara. I leapt for the stick and despite the distance between us I landed on him and pulled him to the ground, pinning him there with my knee to his throat. He choked as he looked up at me. I fought against my sudden surge of hatred toward him. I swallowed and reminded myself of the reason I was even here.

Rain misread my actions as a clear sign of permission to attack. She ran for the cave, her eyes narrowing on the girl. I leapt on Rain, holding Lady Momiko's stick to her throat and pulling her back with it so she would not injure the girl. She grabbed my stick and threw me over her before holding the stick out toward me. I flushed furiously at my own weakness and kicked into her shin to drop her before collecting Lady Momiko's stick from the ground.

I moved quickly to the front of the cave to where the young girl stood screaming. I reached her just as Rain did. My right eye suddenly was exposed to light and I dropped to the ground, covering my eye with my hand to stop the light from bursting into it. Instantly it blinded me and caused such a headache. I looked at Rain, realizing that it was not the girl she was pursuing. The girl was a decoy to distract me so that she could tear off the bandage that concealed my right eye. My heart pounded at my exposed secret. I was unsure if the others had seen. I could not reveal my eye again in the light of day even if I wanted to. Already my mind ached at the flash bomb of brightness. The pain paralyzed me.

Trim jumped in front of me defensively, growling at her. He made no attack on her, as he knew I would not allow it. Rain's orange eyes steadied on me. Now, even in the presence of humans—a potential threat, I will admit—we were wary of our alliance. *How opportunistic of her,* I thought to myself with begrudged admiration.

"Rain!" Fimble yelled at her.

Her black ears pulled back at the sound of his condemning tone. "I cannot let you blindly follow her if she is hiding secrets from us. I do not care about her royal bloodline!" Rain said emotionally, obviously pained by her argument with Fimble.

I looked at Fimble, scared that he might have already seen my defect—the hideous curse with which I had been burdened. If he did, would he want to kill me now? I shrank back into the dark cool dampness of the cave's entrance.

Welcoming the distraction, the human ran for his little sister. He pulled her with him as he edged away from the scene. We all at once noticed the movement so he swung a punch at Trim, who was now the closest to them. Trim easily dodged it without even blinking and knocked the human in the stomach, winding him and taking his breath away so severely it caused him to pass out. The human body was so much more fragile than our own. Instead of catching him, Trim let him drop to the ground. Trim could have easily killed him with one punch, but as the human drew ragged breaths from the ground, I could tell Trim had respected my wishes—somewhat.

The little girl fled for the safety of the cave once again and screamed as her brother fell. I shushed her, still covering my right eye. The cool temperature and darkness of the cave had relieved it. I crawled toward the girl, still hiding my eye from Fimble and Rain who watched me from behind. *They cannot see my face.*

"Shhh, we are not here to hurt you," I said soothingly to the girl. "We are here to look after your brother and you; we will keep you safe."

"No!" she shrieked, piercing my ears. Her wail increased and birds behind us flocked to the sky, startled by the high-pitched squeal. "You hurt us all! You killed my daddy!"

"Sia, this is not the kind of attention we can afford to cause," Trim remarked as he watched the birds gather into a frenzied swarm above our heads. His deep voice only scared the girl even more. We had to settle her down otherwise we were at risk of drawing the attention of a rival wolf, perhaps even one of Taleb's followers. The commotion was certain to arouse suspicion if our enemies were close enough to detect it.

"No, no, no," I whispered gently to her. "We won't hurt you. You see, we are all much more scared of *you*!"

She wiped the tears away from her eyes defiantly. "No, but you are so scary! You hurt us, you have big claws!" She screamed out loud once again and the sound echoed throughout the cave. I looked behind me now, unsettled. If our pursuers heard that or recognized our scents, they would surely follow. It was essential we calmed her at once.

"No, look," I said, revealing my small, filed nails that were certainly not as monstrous as the kind she had just described. Some of our kind did have large claws and could use them as weapons, but mine were not as pointed or fierce. "We will carry you and your brother to safety, but right now we are also scared of those big monsters with the claws... they might even be coming here now."

"No, but I don't want them to come," the little girl sobbed hysterically. I wondered if asking her name would help to calm her. I had never had a little kin and I didn't interact with many cubs as I aged. What kind of words did they want to hear? What could I say to make her trust me?

"We won't let them hurt you, I promise. You can even have Ara by your side the whole time," I slowly brushed over Ara's fur, who was sitting near the little girl with her head on her non-infected shin. I looked at it again, assessing the damage. The flesh around the wound had begun to turn a deep black. If it was not properly treated it would give her blood poisoning within weeks. That was not something I wanted to happen to this innocent young one, even if she was human. Slowly her tears began to trail off and she wiped them away from her face.

I closed my right eye when I felt Fimble's presence enter the cave behind me. "Sia, show me your eye, please," he commanded. His hard tone hurt me and the girl was instantly mistrustful again as she noticed I also hid it from her.

"Trim?" I called, my voice shaky. At that moment I desperately needed his opinion. I wondered if he could deflect Fimble's questions. Or perhaps he thought I should reveal it to them? I felt insecure. I hadn't realized how deeply my eye would affect my confidence in leading other wolves. This was a Phantom Wolf's eye—the eye of a creature that was both hunted and condemned. Our kind feared humans so much that they would quickly try to sever the bond between the cursed wolf and the human. Would they turn on me in such a way? Would Fimble want to kill me?

"Do not ask her," Trim said harshly, picking up the human male. "Return her bandage."

"It is not that I ask her to bare her very soul, only what she is hiding from us here and now. I know that you deplore lies, Sia, and that you are an honest wolf. I cannot help but be offended that you now would shroud yourself in secrecy."

Fimble's words felt as though they had scraped my heart. The girl still looked at me with suspense and wariness. Without looking at Fimble I knew that his expression must mirror hers. He was right; I had begun to turn into a secretive wolf—a trait that I hated most. I let my hand drop to the dirt floor of the cave, blinking vigorously even in the shade. I looked once more at the human to remind myself of my mission. Her skin was a transparent white. Even her golden hair and the odd material she wore over her skin were washed out because of the vision I was afforded by my right eye. I took a deep breath and rose to my feet.

I turned to face Fimble. If I wanted him to help me protect the humans then I had to tell him the truth. Although we all feared the humans, I needed him to understand that if anyone was at risk, it was me. Although I was at a distinct advantage because of my premonitions and instinct, I was also at the greatest risk from persecution. I already had a Phantom Wolf eye. Who knew the repercussions of being so close to a human? I did not know how I had obtained The Great Phantom Wolf's eye. She had become known as 'The Great' after she was deceased, but many still feared her. How would they react to know that her eye was within me?

Fimble's mouth tightened as he stared at my right eye. The sun behind him pierced through the opening of the cave, blinding me. The pain was far too great for me to handle and I lifted my hand to shield myself from the light. I could not properly see him but I could sense that he was moving closer to me, but slowly. His hand reached for me and I did not flinch as he touched my face. His rough hand cupped my jaw as he assessed my eye closely and then his finger trailed over my lips. I didn't understand his assessment.

"What is it?" he asked simply, his tone unrecognizable.

"I think I have been cursed with a Phantom Wolf's eye," I bravely said, unsure of how he would react to such a controversial statement.

"Does it hurt you?"

"Only during the day," I said, dropping my gaze from his.

He placed his thumb beneath my chin to raise my face upward. "Thank you for showing this to me, Sia. I understand it has dealt you great pain and caused you anguish, so thank you for trusting me. Your secret is safe with me."

I instinctively hugged him, so relieved to have his acceptance. I blinked back my tears. Fimble's hands clasped together behind my back as he accepted my embrace. "Thank you," I whispered into his chest. A burden was lifted from my heart. I now knew another could stand by my side, even though I had this defect. I pulled away, wiping at the few tears that had escaped.

Trim's jaw was tight. Although his face was the picture of studied indifference, when I met his eye, I saw resentment. I did not know if he was angry because I had told Fimble about my eye, or if he simply objected to me hugging whom he perceived to be the enemy.

Rain walked into the mouth of the cave, offering the bandage to me. I fumbled to grab it out of her hand, disorientated by my enhanced vision. "We need to go now," she said fiercely. "It seems as though your squealing human has drawn attention to us."

Chapter Twenty-One- Broken Innocence

"$\mathscr{P}$ick the girl up," I instructed Fimble. I quickly wrapped the bandage around my eye so I could see properly once again. I crouched in front of her, holding her arms gently. "We must leave now so we can protect you and your brother. But you *must* stay quiet."

"Sia, they are not that far from here, leave the humans," Trim growled fiercely.

"You will carry him on your back," I said authoritatively.

Fimble assessed the little girl cautiously. He gently picked her up, trying not to directly touch her skin. He settled her so that he was carrying her on his back, and she nestled her face into his long gray hair.

"This way," Rain said, ushering us out of the cave and back toward where we had originally come from. We ran into that direction. Already the scents of the others were more noticeable. Rain speedily climbed up one of the trees ahead of us, assessing the distance between us and them. "There are many, perhaps forty," she called down in a discouraged tone.

"Sia, you must take the girl," Fimble said, handing Reina over to me. I gathered her weight, surprised to find that she was actually a lot heavier than she first appeared. I assumed that because they were so fragile they would not weigh very much.

"Why, where will you go?" I asked, frantic. Fimble began climbing up a tree further away from us. It had the same height as the one that Rain was perched in, her bow and arrows in hand. Fimble quickly settled into his position. He too gathered the bow and arrows from his back. It became rapidly apparent that they intended to ambush the first few who came toward us.

Trim and I ran with the humans, Ara beside me keeping pace. The scents overwhelmed us. From behind we could hear vicious snarls and whimpers as the arrows reached their targets. But not all the scents were behind us. Trim and I noticed at once that their smells surrounded us. How had we come so close to our pursuers without detecting them before now?

Trim shattered the roof of a large hollow log that was covered in moss. "Get in," he ordered, placing the girl inside. Next to her he set down the unconscious male that now stirred. I placed Ara in her lap and began covering it with branches. Trim firmly grabbed my hand, stopping me. "You need to hide in there too."

"I am not leaving you," I choked.

"I am not asking you too. Your goal was to protect the humans. The moss will cover your scents. If the male human wakes up he will react badly and make noise in there. You must be in there to calm him and silence him or they will kill the girl as well," Trim explained, pushing me into the log. I understood his reasoning but I did not want him to fight on his own. I had to trust him and his judgment, just as he did mine with the humans. I slithered into the log. The little girl was holding her mouth as she tried to quieten her sobs. "It's okay," I soothed her. Even though the log had moss on it I could already feel that it was not going to be enough to cover our scents. The snapping of nearby sticks began and I feared the beautiful forest that we were currently in would become bloodstained if it were only Trim who fought against so many.

The more I wanted to be able to hide us, the lighter I felt. The male human stirred and mumbled as nearby growls and calls began. He awoke and saw me, and the surprise caused him to hit his head on the interior of the log. I indicated for him to be silent.

He looked at our surroundings and immediately grasped our situation. I hoped now he would understand I was not the enemy.

I felt hazy as I wanted to hide our presence, so much so that I wanted our scents gone. I felt tired focusing on such a thing. My body reacted oddly. I held the girl closely in protectiveness. Screams rang out as Trim fought the wolves off. I felt even more protective of the humans as the horrific screams penetrated our ears.

I realized then that, because of me, our scents no longer existed. Lady Momiko had once told me of the gift that Sia, the Phantom Wolf, had had. She could smother her scent and no one was able to detect her location. To my surprise, I realized I was doing the same. The eye she had given me encompassed far more gifts than I had realized.

Reina screamed when a male wolf shattered the top of the log, revealing where we hid. I pushed Reina toward her brother, threw Ara back, and then jumped out of the log and onto the man. I kicked him away from the log. I could now see the many wolves that crept from the trees surrounding us. They were already prepared with weapons and savage snarls.

"There she is!" one of the female wolves exclaimed, pointing at me. I sensed the two humans and Ara behind me cowering further into the log. I hoped none of the wolves could see or smell them.

Trim came by my side with his knife in his hand. He was unable to protect me from any particular direction as they encircled us. I growled savagely, holding onto Lady Momiko's stick. I held her moonstone in my other hand. Trim began attacking the wolves on his right, slicing at their throats. I used my stick as my weapon, smashing it over the head of one of the oncoming wolves. Quickly I prodded it behind me into another wolf's stomach. I knelt as one tried to slash at my throat and then used my stick to force him away.

I held my stick firmly to the ground and then flipped over it to jump away from where an arrow shot at me. My keen hearing was now so precise and my reflexes so quick that I could calculate which direction the arrow would go in just by the sound of the archer drawing the arrow back.

Two wolves sized me up at the same time. I balanced on my feet carefully, anticipating their steps as they approached me. I blocked their attack using Lady Momiko's stick. Another attacked me from behind but he was pounced on by Trim. I jumped back as one leapt off a giant log for me. She kicked Lady Momiko's stick out of my hand but I still clutched onto the moonstone, bracing myself for hand-to-hand combat. The woman tried to cut me with a small knife and she grazed it past my arm. I took the wound to bait her then grasped her arm. I punched fiercely into her elbow and grazed my thin claws across her wrist. It bled fiercely and the woman howled as she retreated, holding her broken arm.

I was always small in size, but my speed was faster than that of most other wolves. Trim had always taught me to use my size against my opponent. Two wolves wrestled Trim. One pinned Trim's arms behind his back as the other went to swipe the sword across his stomach. I jumped on his arm, grabbing it firmly enough that he could push it no further into the direction of Trim. The large, overfed wolf grabbed me by the back of my hair and pulled me to him. I bit savagely into his arm. I was disgusted in myself for doing it, but it forced him to drop his hold on me. I spat the grotesque taste out of my mouth, the filth making me gag.

The human male picked up my stick and used it as a weapon. Lady Momiko's stick swung over the wolf's head. The wolf looked at him in horror and rage, instantly recognizing him as human. This one human could destroy the wolf's entire pack. If the human were to kill him or any of us, we would be cursed as Phantom Wolves and we would slaughter our own pack. The power this one human had against us instantly struck fear into the eyes of this rival wolf.

I took advantage of his startled position and jumped on his back, pulling him away by the ears. The wolf thrashed back and forth. I elbowed him in the neck three times but with little success until Trim came and stabbed him in the throat while I held him back. I jumped away from his plummeting body so he did not fall on me.

Trim threw the knife toward me, taking me by surprise. The blade glided past my face, hitting the wolf behind me. Only a few now surrounded; their numbers had depleted rapidly. The few that edged toward us were quickly shot down by arrows. I looked over the wolves that lay dead or severely injured on the ground, the smell of blood already rising in the air. Rain and Fimble revealed themselves. They were both bloodied and scratched.

"Are you okay?" Trim asked me, assessing me. His face and shoulder bled profusely, much to my concern. I knew he would dismiss his injuries.

The human male pulled Reina out and hugged her to him tenderly. She cried in his arms. I was relieved to see that she was okay and that the male was also unscathed.

"Thank you," I said my voice reaching out to the human who fought with us. He had been considered the enemy for many years and yet when we were both attacked by our own kind, he had protected Trim and me. Whom should we fear most: the humans or our own kind? They would turn on us so quickly because of Taleb's wrath.

I collected Lady Momiko's stick, understanding now why she had given it to me. I could use it to not only hold myself up when I was weakened by premonitions, but also as a weapon. It was not deadly enough to kill anyone but it gave me the means to protect myself. Did she foresee that I would hesitate to kill—that a knife would be pointless in my gentle hands?

The male human walked over to us steadily, holding Reina's hand. She looked over all the bodies with wide terrified eyes. I wished that somehow I could have saved her from seeing such a scene.

"They came from a nearby camp," Rain said, wiping over her chest. She had sustained an injury during the battle. A deep cut above her knee forced her to limp when she walked. Even though it looked painful, she acted like she had not even noticed it.

"They're guarding our ships," the male human said directly to me.

"What is a 'ship'?" Fimble asked. He seemed relatively unharmed, only his long gray hair was messy.

The human looked at us all oddly, as though we were the outsiders because we did not know what this "ship" was. *He* was the other-worldly one.

"Um, I guess in a simple explanation, you can travel on water by it. It is made out of materials like wood that can float," he described.

"Lyon, tell them about Daddy," Reina cried, tugging on the material that covered his chest. So, he was named "Lyon." He looked upset at the mention of his father, as though he could not bring himself to speak. I remembered Reina mentioning through her tears that her father was killed by my kind.

"With such a thing Taleb could easily cross The Great Water into the Forbidden Land," Fimble thought out loud. I thought about it for a moment. Such an object would need to camp near the water's edge. I sniffed in the direction of where our attackers had originally come from. Were we near The Great Water?

"I know where we are," Rain said, answering my unvoiced question. "And half of those who attacked us had the same colored fur and scent of my own pack."

"My father had suspicions that Taleb and his followers had made a small camp there, where his followers stayed," Fimble said, answering more unspoken questions. He and Rain quickly evaluated the situation. "I guess this is the reason why they stayed so close. Perhaps Taleb knew of these 'ships.'"

"How did they get these?" I asked, confused how Taleb intended to utilize a human object.

After much hesitation Lyon spoke up. "Every year a large group comprised of my father, friends, and family went on a cruise. We would look for beaches to stay on and celebrate for no particular reason. We had already come to this island twice before," Lyon explained, breaking eye contact with me to look down on his sister's golden head. "But this year, we were all attacked. No one else is left."

Reina began to cry, hiding her face in her brother's stomach once again. I felt such hatred for what my kind had done to both him and Reina. How could Taleb slaughter so many innocent beings? But looking around me I realized he cared for neither human nor wolf.

"How many of these ships did they take possession of?" Fimble asked, assessing Rain's injuries.

"Four," Lyon stated. "Our father protected us and tried to fight them off, but it was as if they already knew we were coming to that exact beach at that time. We never usually went to the same beach consecutively, but my father and the others loved this place so much that they continued to visit it. It makes me think that they were watching us in the previous years that we came. Shortly after we escaped we ran into you for the first time. I found that cave and we have hid in it ever since."

"I wonder what they did with so many human bodies," Rain said inconsiderately. They were not *just* humans. To these two they were family.

"Large billows of smoke came from the same place that same evening, I assume they burned them all," Lyon said picking up his little sister and holding her close to him as her wailing became louder.

"You are very brave," I said to him. I wanted to offer him my condolences; they had already lost so much. But we had to make a plan. "We must destroy those ships. If Taleb learns how to use them he will fetch humans and bring them back to us so he can threaten us with them."

"I don't believe so, if he had wanted that he wouldn't have killed all the humans, he would have just captured them and used them against us," Fimble pointed out.

"But he didn't kill them all," Trim reasoned. We looked at the two human survivors of the massacre. "What Taleb wants is not to control these humans, but to visit the Forbidden Land. Could you imagine the control he would have of our kind if he threatened that against us? He would be able to take as many humans as he wanted, at any time. He is after these two to show him how to use the ships for a far greater gain."

It quickly fell into place why Taleb would have so many wolves near the ships. They were there not only to guard them, but to watch out in case these humans came back. They followed not our scents but the humans'. A shiver ran down my spine. I felt like I was in the presence of Lady Momiko; it was as if she were there to guide me with each step I took. "This is why she wanted us to protect them," I realized. They were the only weapon we had against Taleb.

I looked into the sky at the faint outline of the moon. *Tonight is the full moon.* I looked at Lady Momiko's moonstone that I held firmly in my hand. *Can I try to make contact with Lady Momiko tonight for guidance on what to do next?*

"We must burn the ships," Rain said, walking into that direction.

"No!" both Lyon and I shouted at the same time.

"That is our only way to return home," Lyon added.

"We need to regroup and tend to our wounds. I would like to try and connect to my Spirit Pack tonight for guidance. I am not entirely sure if I can do it yet, but I believe Lady Momiko has given me this gift so that I can make contact," I reasoned, looking at Trim with uneasiness. I was trying to convince both them and myself at the same time that we could rely on my ability. I wasn't even sure if I possessed such a gift but it was the only thing I could focus my mind on after everything that had happened recently: my illness, eye, premonitions, and betrayals. I grasped onto this, believing in it and hoping that with such ability I could be of some use.

"Is it Lady Momiko who gifted you with sight or only because you have a Phantom Wolf's eye?" asked Rain. I felt vulnerable and stripped bare by her words.

"Rain!" Fimble interjected angrily. "We will rest for tonight, and depending on what happens tonight, tomorrow we will burn those ships. I trust Sia, and if she only asks for one night, then I will permit that."

I thanked Fimble for taking charge of the situation and giving me a small time frame to try and prove myself. I was glad we were united, despite my curse. He was still willing to stay and fight beside us to protect the humans. Now it seemed we all agreed on why the humans should be contained away from Taleb.

"You're safest with us," I reassured Lyon. He was looking at Ara. She wagged her tail at him in a comforting gesture of reassurance.

"Sia, let's go," Trim commanded, indicating that we should follow Fimble and Rain. One of his hands rested on my shoulder. His hands were warm despite the chilly day. My eyes strayed to the humans behind me. I feared the impact walking through the dead bodies would have on Reina. I was worried we had already broken her innocence.

Chapter Twenty-Two- Human Curiosity

We put as much distance between us and the battle ground as possible, knowing that soon others would come across the bodies and alert the remainder of Taleb's followers.

I explained to Trim as we fled that I thought I could use my ability to smolder our scents. He didn't seem overly surprised. He had known Sia to use such a skill. A few wolves could do it and she was the only Phantom Wolf who could. He explained other abilities she had, such as being able to transfer her physical body to another place. He said that after her fight with Kiba in his Phantom Wolf state, she was able to use that ability to drop into the very same room I had revealed behind the library—the one where she killed her human, Thomas, and attacked Taleb.

Lyon carried Reina on his back. She was obviously exhausted by such a horrific morning. I couldn't help but constantly look at the wound on her shin as I knew that she needed aid. Did human bodies function differently to ours? I wondered if our healing methods would work. My mother and Lady Momiko had taught me much about the use of remedial herbs and wound cleansing. Maybe she needed to go back to her own land for the correct cure.

I was glad that Lyon had taken them to the cave with the heavy minerals that hid their scent away from Taleb, but we could not hide them in that same place again. Although we were safer here than we were in the open, they were still so vulnerable. We had a very small party in comparison to Taleb's vast one.

Trim, Rain, and Fimble were all fine warriors. All of them were the best I had ever seen. I grew embarrassed when I remembered that I had once considered myself on the same par as them, as if I were as strong or skillful. I now realized after a journey of self-discovery that I was as fragile as everyone had once claimed. Perhaps strong-mindedness did not equate to strength. That was proved especially true while we were being hunted.

Reina slept for most the day. After many hours we came across a valley near a small watering hole that was full of moss. We could rely on it to cover our scents somewhat. My stomach growled loudly but I dismissed Trim when he offered me a fresh kill. I would find a way to eat, but still I could not accept the thought of ripping into a freshly killed creature's flesh. When Reina awoke, she blinked at the sunshine in confusion before she began playing with Ara, who was unfazed by the human's smell or presence. I watched Lyon calculatingly as he supervised his sibling. I edged myself closer and closer to him, much to Trim's disgruntlement.

"How old are you?" I asked Lyon curiously.

He looked at Fimble and Trim shiftily before answering me. "Twenty," Lyon responded. "And you?"

"Eighteen," I replied, recalling my lack of celebration for it. I thought of all those wolves that would have danced on my birthday as I lay curled in my bed. It was surreal to think that the majority of those wolves would now be dead.

"Only eighteen? And you are royalty? And these are like, your guards or something? Or—"

"It is a long story," I interrupted quickly. Trim's and Fimble's ears had pulled back at his words. No doubt they were both very interested to hear which of them meant something more to me. "Would you say you are the average size for a fully-grown, male human?"

Although he seemed to be of the same size and height as our average male wolves, he was so much weaker. He was lacking in hair and fur which led me to believe the material he wore over his body was perhaps there to keep him warm. The only thing that adorned my body was the silver band that draped over my neck and chest—the one that Trim had given to me for my birthday. I fiddled with the moonstone at my chest. Lyon's eyes lowered to the moonstone before he quickly looked up, as if guilty of something. He flushed red.

"Can you please wear this?" he asked, startling me by taking the material off his chest. It had one large hole for his head to poke through, and another two for his arms. "I find it... *distracting* that you are not wearing clothing," Lyon blushed.

My understanding of the human mind was lacking—I could not fathom why he would bestow upon me such an impractical gift. "What is this for?" I asked, accepting the material in my hands and looking over the orange-colored material with interest.

"You will not wear that," Trim grumbled. He snatched it out of my hand and threw it back toward Lyon. "*You* will keep it to yourself."

Lyon's face hardened and he grinded his teeth before pulling the material back onto his body. "It is called a 'shirt,'" Lyon announced. "We *humans* do not walk around naked like your kind; it would be improper and inappropriate."

"We are... 'naked'? You are not used to 'naked'?" I asked, awed that there could be a land where they all wore this material simply because... it was expected of them? My ears pulled back at the images in my mind. How much material they would have to make! Lyon again grew red in the cheeks while I pondered it. He made me feel conscious like I was doing something wrong. He did not answer my question which led me to believe that perhaps the answer was a secret for humans, or maybe only him.

"I am sorry but we do not wear 'shirts,'" I said, enjoying the thrill of exploring the human culture. "I hope this will not deter you from interacting further with us. I am most interested in learning more about how humans conduct themselves."

"Sia," Trim warned, "Lay your curiosity down, it is almost nighttime. You need your rest if you are going to try to connect with your Spirit Pack for the first time."

"And he is only your *guard*?" Lyon whispered to me, dismissing Trim's words as quickly as I did. I found humor in his words but Trim was growing angry that we both ignored him. It seemed Lyon and I were just as curious about one another.

"I have known Trim since I was born; he has always looked over me," I whispered back. I looked back at Trim as I spoke, startled at the realization that he was technically only my "guard." My feelings for him were so raw it made the title ridiculous. For so long I had tried to impress him. I had wanted to be his mate. Now I tried to push those feelings aside—I had to.

"Sia," Trim growled under his breath.

I could understand why Trim would want to disrupt our conversation. Trim had always hated humans, perhaps more than most. They were the reason why Sia faced a premature death. Now we had them as companions and he was very agitated within their presence, despite the fact that they weren't a threat to us at all. Reina was clearly young and in my eyes harmless. If anyone were a threat it was Lyon, but I very much doubted he was capable of any wrongdoing.

I noticed when Lyon put his shirt back on that there was a thick brown band around his neck. I reached out to touch it, curious. Lyon flinched and Trim grabbed my hand away from him, his expression insinuating that I was not to touch.

"It is a necklace," Lyon said after much hesitation. He placed his hand on the same object I had been reaching for. "Much like the silver string and gems you have on your chest."

I looked at the moonstone on my chest in a new light. *"Necklace,"* I repeated, exploring how the word felt on my tongue.

"Sia," Trim grumbled again. Finally I listened to him, knowing that he would not stop. If I were to continue any longer he would physically carry me away from the conversation. It would not be the first time he had done so.

"I will rest now," I agreed. Ara followed me to the base of a tree. Trim followed behind and then sat down next to me. I folded myself around Ara on the hard ground, my tail flickering back and forth with anticipation. I was putting so much pressure on myself for this to go well tonight. But I doubted myself; I was scared that I would fail everyone, and myself.

"Everything will be all right," Trim said, looking ahead.

"I am scared I will fail everyone tonight and hinder us in some way," I admitted, looking at his orange tail, which was still. His fur waved in the light breeze.

"You have never doubted yourself like that; it is not in your nature," Trim teased.

"I have learned much about myself from this, and I am truly scared for not only myself but for everyone else: my pack that I abandoned, my parents whose location I do not know, you, the others that are here with us. I realize now that I am not as strong as I had once thought. Everyone was right about me. I don't know who I truly am anymore."

I stared at his tail, embarrassed by my feelings. I had insinuated that I knew what I was doing tonight. I would try to contact Lady Momiko, but what if I had jeopardized everyone's lives just because I believed I was right?

"You are strong, in your own way," Trim said, patting his hand over mine comfortingly. "You must rest now."

I looked up at him with my left eye, comforted by his touch and kind words. It was foreign to me for him to be so kind when I was so used to his scornful looks and tongue. I wrapped my tail around Ara. With Trim's large hand held firmly over mine, I fell into a fitful sleep.

Chapter Twenty-Three- Moment of Confessions

When I awoke the moon was blazing strongly and more beautifully than it usually did at a full moon. Trim still sat by my side, looking as though he hadn't moved the whole time I had slept. His hand was still on mine. His blue eye glistened in the moon's shine as he admired the night sky.

My stomach growled with hunger. I knew most wolves would not have an issue with ripping into an animal's lifeless body. I knew I infuriated Trim because I could not yet eat in such a way. He probably thought I was being dramatic as usual. But I just couldn't bring myself to do it.

I looked over to Rain and saw that she had wrapped around her knee a thick vine, which had helped in stopping the bleeding. She looked slightly discolored by the amount of blood she had lost. I remembered she had told me of her self-sufficiency after being left alone in nature. Fimble filed pointed branches nearby, creating wooden arrows. His pouch was running low on the silver tipped ones. Reina still slept with her head on Lyon's lap.

Near to our group there was a rock large enough for me to climb. I would see the moon brilliantly from such an angle. I did not know how to communicate with my Spirit Pack or even if there were any specific requirements for making contact with them. I grabbed Lady Momiko's walking stick and her moonstone, recalling her intrusive questions on our last meeting. I hoped that everything we had talked of was leading to this place and time, and that she could give us the guidance that we needed for tomorrow's events.

We all had reached an understanding about destroying the ships and confronting Taleb's men that guarded them. My body shuddered at the thought. *We could all lose our lives because of it,* I thought gravely. This is why I had to be accurate. This was my only way to protect them. I had to find a way to connect with Lady Momiko and her wise words.

I pointed out to Trim the large rock, "Up there." At least there on the rock I would be hidden from the others. If I failed, I would not have to immediately face them with disappointing answers. I could hide on that rock. Trim and I walked up and I sat in a position that did not allow the others to see me. It was only Trim, Ara, and I. I sat on the rock cross-legged, feeling stupid for what I was trying to do. *Do I call out loud for her? Do I hold her rock above my head? Do I need to rattle the bells on her stick and do some kind of dance?*

"Just relax," Trim said gently.

I looked into his stern blue eye and focused on breathing in and out. I held Lady Momiko's moonstone in my hand, thinking of her and trying to push away all the other conflicting thoughts.

"*You have grown much, my little one,*" Lady Momiko's voice rang through my ears.

My eyes burst open in shock that I had heard her voice. My black ears pinned back while I tried to refocus and listen to her again. "*Lady Momiko?*"

"*Yes,*" her crisp voice replied somewhat mockingly, suggesting that I was foolish to ask.

"*I can really speak to you?*" I asked almost tearfully.

"*You can speak to me whenever I wish to speak to you. If I have nothing to say I will not come,*" she said impatiently.

"Why can I not see you?" I asked, searching the darkness of my mind.

"Who wants to see an old bag of bones like me?" she laughed.

I smiled to see that her humor was preserved in the afterlife before continuing with, *"Taleb, he—"*

"I know all about Taleb, as does Sia and Kiba here. We have given you the tools you need to defeat him, but we cannot do much more for you now, my little one."

My mind roamed as I thought of Sia and Kiba being so close. When I focused on other things I felt the connection between Lady Momiko and me drop in strength. I had to focus on our conversation completely. *"Why did you give me this gift, and why has Sia cursed me with her eye?"* I demanded.

"Like most things, you will find out in due time. Sometimes, my young one, even if we can see the future we cannot demand all the answers. You would try to change it, which would lead to more disastrous actions. Everything that will happen is meant to be."

"Please, Lady Momiko! Our home, our pack, even our very land is in danger because of Taleb. Surely you must know that!" I flushed angrily.

"I do not wish to repeat my words again, my little one. You remember the words I spoke when I gave you the first two of your gifts? Everything that I told you was to lead you to what I truly wanted you to focus on. You may have grown in certain ways, but you do not yet fully understand."

"But what do we do? I can't fail them!" I gasped desperately.

"You will do what everyone has already agreed on. You cannot call on me to give you strength, you need to find your

own," her voice quietened into a whisper and I knew she had walked away from me.

Tears built in my eyes. I wiped them away, mortified. Although she had confirmed her gift had passed over to me, she would not aid me. I could not help the others. I was useless in so many ways. This was the one thing I could have done for them and I had failed.

"Sia?" Trim asked, crouching beside me.

I stared at the hard ground, ashamed that I had learned nothing from the conversation. Lady Momiko only spoke in riddles. "She won't help us," I admitted, my voice shaking. In that moment I despised Lady Momiko. Was it because she was in the afterlife that she did not care? I supposed it was no longer her obligation to help her pack. "I have this stupid curse that I cannot use! I have a 'gift' that has proved useless. I can't even protect myself!" I had to yell the words to release the deepest thoughts that haunted me. If I said them in front of Trim, would he not realize then that they were better off without me?

"Sia," Trim said sternly, trying to grasp my attention.

I threw my arms in the air, my mind finally breaking. "I had one thing to do, one thing I could have possibly done to aid everyone, but I'm useless!" I bellowed, throwing Lady Momiko's stick at the wall of rock behind me. Trim reached out for me, trying to get a firm hold on my arms to curb my tantrum, but I took several steps back. *"You* don't even believe I can defend myself!"

I thought of all my years of hard training. He had stayed close to protect me, constantly reminding me that he needed to be there in case I needed strength. Apparently it was so obvious to everyone but me that strength was what I lacked. No one believed I had it. No one believed in *me*. How could I have been so foolish to judge others for "misinterpreting" me when I was the epitome of weakness? I had misjudged myself. "You never thought me strong!" I whimpered with tears rolling down my face.

He pushed me toward the wall so I could not run away from him like I usually did. I felt like I was splitting in two. I was so unsure of myself and now I was losing myself in my tears. Never would I have allowed Trim to see me like this, but I had nothing to hide behind any longer: no Siesta, no parents, and no self-righteous attitude. But I wouldn't run away because I didn't want to be the one coward in this hopeless situation.

"Sia, you are getting worked up," he said. He seemed oddly fired up himself. His chest rose and fell quickly.

"You would have usually taunted me by now! Told me I was being cubbish and selfish! Am I no longer even deserving of your scorn? Am I too pathetic a creature to taunt?" I gasped. Anxiety swept over me and I doubled over, clutching at my ribs as I tried to breathe.

"You are putting too much pressure on yourself. You cannot fix all this by yourself. None of this was your doing," Trim whispered.

I raised one hand to push him away from me but he pinned my arm against the hard surface behind me. I ripped the bandage off my eye with my other hand, revealing my green eye. I was so sick of holding my words back. Now I wanted my deepest thoughts exposed. I could force him to turn his back on me once and for all by speaking the truth. "You would rather it were her here with you, wouldn't you? You would rather be looking into her green eyes and face! *She* would not whimper; she would protect you. She would bite into an animal's flesh. I have her eye and her gift and yet I cannot be her! I cannot protect you or anyone else—"

Trim's other hand suddenly pinned my waist hard against the wall, shocking me into silence. His breath quickly took my own and his lips pressed hungrily against mine, his tongue enticing me. His body pressed firmly against mine. His lips were so soft in comparison to the rest of his exterior. The warmth from his mouth spread quickly throughout my entire body.

He pulled back and looked at me intensely through his blue eye. I stared back at him, unsure of what had just happened. "You always push me," he growled, panting hard. He pressed himself against me, kissing me fervently once again. His tongue took the lead, inviting me to kiss him passionately. He released his hold on my hand and I pushed my hand through his orange hair, trying to pull him closer. My other hand coiled around his neck. My desperate tears had turned into a hunger I could not control.

His heart beat rapidly within his hard chest, forcing my desire as I grasped the extent of his own. I wrapped my legs around his waist and he held me up against the hard rock, his strong arms supporting my weight. I kissed his lips, his cheeks, his neck, and then found his lips again eagerly. My legs tightened around him fiercely. My body had an erotic urge and desperation like I had never experienced before.

He pulled away as I tugged on his lips. He rested his forehead on mine, panting as heavily as I did for our lost breath. I so desperately wanted him. My arms shivered when I looked into his blue eye. I inhaled his hot breath.

"You always push me," he repeated, "Until I cannot contain myself anymore."

"So you do not see her instead of me?" I asked stupidly. His actions alone should have been enough to prove to me where his desire lay. But the doubt still lingered in my mind. Trim stroked my cheek and then under my eye, wiping away my previous tears. I had forgotten what I had even cried about; my mind raced as frantically as my heart.

"It is not her I want, Sia. It is *you* I need." He stroked his thumb over my right eyelid, closing it gently. My remaining eye mirrored his blue one. We stared at each other. Each was imperfect, yet somehow together we were whole. My unmatched eye and his missing one were irrelevant when we gazed at one another. "It does not matter if you have Sia's eye. I will always only ever see you."

Trim pressed his lips against mine again. His kiss lingered on my lips, no longer fast or hot but reassuring and caring—loving, even. He dropped his head so I could not look at his face and guess what he was thinking. "So, it is okay if I do this? Even if I look like I do, and I am how I am?" He now went red across his cheeks.

I found myself also hiding a slight smile as I wondered if this was the reason he had held himself back from me for so long; he seemed almost shy. "This is all I've ever wanted you to do." I kissed the scarring of his eye and then his lips again, still shaky.

"I need to cool down, right now," he said honestly. I understood what he meant; my own body was still trembling with desire. I could have begged him for more, but I wanted this moment to be exactly what it was. Our moment of confessions.

Trim lowered my small figure gently down to the ground. My legs almost buckled because of their weakness. He smiled and guided me back up before standing back against the wall, breathing heavily. His tail was flicking wildly. I stood against him with my back to him and we both stared up at the moon, trying to process what had just happened. Trim wrapped his arm around my shoulders, pulling me closer into him. I rested my head against his chest.

"I never thought of you as without strength. I just had to better myself so I could be worthy of being by your side. But like I have always said, I will always be beside you to protect you. Not out of obligation, but for this," he said, stroking my neck.

It was the purest his words had ever been. I only pitied the circumstances that had forced him to reveal them to me. "Just for now, before we go back to the others, I would like to stay like this for a moment."

Trim kissed my black ear and then the top of my head as Ara curled up beside me. Together all three of us enjoyed one another's company, trying to ignore the fact that the fateful day ahead would soon be upon us.

Chapter Twenty-Four- My Equal

I fell asleep peacefully in Trim's arms. I did not have reoccurring visions of the things I had witnessed on my journey to this place. In his arms I felt warm and safe, like the promise he had always made me. His words eased me and I knew that he had done all that he had to protect me. My heart raced to know our feelings were the same. Not only did he believe in me, but he saw me as the woman I had been trying to prove to him that I was for so long now. Perhaps I had to grow more, to face my own internal defeat, and break down my own arrogance, before he could approach me. I had lost much but gained in so many other ways. I now knew my own limitations and I had Trim by my side too.

I was fearful for my parents but I knew they were too clever to be found. We had many guards who would protect them with their lives if necessary. Perhaps at Siesta's warning they had escaped. My mind tore when I thought of Siesta—I had walked away from her murderer. I was enraged to know so many had been killed because of Taleb's words. He would kill any wolf in his way. What sickened me the most were the wolves that would follow him blindly, simply because their Alpha's dictated that they should. I feared for the humans too as we created a plan of strategy. They had to be so close to us as they were almost defenseless against those who would try to capture them or even worse, kill them.

I patted Ara vigorously while Trim fed her a dead bird. At the sight of her meal I felt sick. My stomach curled at the realization that I hadn't eaten for days. I would have to find something to cure me of my inability to eat in such a way. It was only my mental state that forbade me to do so; it would be my next challenge to overcome. I could not disappoint Trim anymore, and I could not starve myself either.

Time was something that we did not have in our favor. The longer we left it, the more time Taleb had to build his guards around the ships, and the more strength we would have to muster from within ourselves to rise against him. We needed to break through their defenses and supply the humans with this ship so they could leave this place once and for all.

Trim suggested we kill them now so we were guaranteed that no more humans would come back. But Lyon understood our predicament, and I trusted in his words when he said he would not speak of this place when he returned to his world. Fimble and Rain created their own secondary plan. If we were to fail, one of them would shoot the humans down so they could not be used against our kind. Time was of the essence and we could not delay any longer to gather familiar warriors. This was something we had to achieve ourselves before we approached my pack again.

We all walked as one through the foliage and mighty trees toward The Great Water. This battle would be one of many if we could not find Taleb. If we could not stop the ships then our land would be divided by a territorial war, one that could last for many years as he claimed back the Kingdom. We now had the opportunity to reinstate my parents' rightful rule over our kind. I faced the fact that I may not see my parents again, though I choked on the thought. I pained to think I might never have the chance to stabilize my home and strengthen the bond between Trim and me.

We shuffled beside one another as if nothing had happened between us but Fimble's agitated brown eyes continued to rest on me unhappily. Fimble had once proclaimed his interest toward me and back then I suspected trickery behind his words. But he was an honest wolf and every word he said to me now was pure and truthful. I sincerely hoped that he did not pine for me or desire that I become his mate.

Rain obviously struggled now despite trying to hide her limp. We were getting closer and I could smell the salty water. The humans trailed behind us, their eyes sunken from a terrible night's sleep. Their skin looked pale because of our cooler atmosphere. They were not conditioned to survive in our environment. Fimble had collected a few weapons after our ambush and he gave them to Lyon and even little Reina.

I wished I could hide them but they pushed forward like they were marching to their deaths. I would protect them. I had to. It was, after all, my instinct that had discovered them. But their lives, just like ours, were without guarantees. Our lives were not safe. We could only fight and hope that we would emerge victorious from the bloody battleground before us.

Fimble sniffed the air around us and then raised his hand to gesture that we should halt. He looked to his right. It was a lone scent, a familiar one. Trim held me back when I stepped forward toward it. My heart had instantly hardened and I was ready to kill. Fiesca's scent lingered and Fimble assessed her exact location, but he let her walk toward us.

"What have you come here for, Fiesca?" Fimble asked harshly.

"You should have not come here," she warned. "Taleb will have you killed."

The memory of her dropping Siesta through the open wall burned my eyes and I was once again witness to her horrific, underserved death. Fiesca was a murderer, a beast. She had no right to live over all those whom she had killed. The innocence of my pack was destroyed because of the bloodlust she harbored.

"They are human," she said, mesmerized by Lyon, who hid Reina behind him. Surprisingly she did not step forward threateningly; perhaps Taleb has ordered that his followers should not kill the remaining humans. But I wondered how many would heed such a dangerous request. The presence of humans was a threat to all wolves alike. If given the chance I imagined some would still try to kill them; after all, they were more of a threat than Taleb's words and wrath. We all readied ourselves for her attack, but she did not challenge us.

"Have you come to kill us?" Fimble interrogated.

Fiesca looked at her brother distantly. "I do remember our mother, Fimble, and after the words you shed the day you became a traitor I have been forced to evaluate a lot. But my hands have too much blood on them to repent. So I simply wanted to ask you to remember me as the kin I once was when we were younger. I will not stand against you today. But if we meet again, if any of our pack, or our father or brother meets with you, we will kill you. But today we are hiding away from you. Your next actions will prove to us where your loyalty truly lies," Fiesca said in a quiet voice. She assessed our small group again before walking away as if she had dignity. She called over her shoulder, "Walk away, Fimble, this fight is not one you can win."

Fimble watched over his sister for a long time. I shadowed my face. Trim looked surprised by the vicious snarls I could not contain. I had not yet told him what she had done to Siesta. I could not let the words pass my lips because it would only make it real. I held back from following her, remembering how Fimble had pleaded with me once before to let his sister go. Tomorrow I would not heed those words.

Fimble had lost much as well. By choosing to not take my life he was now traitor to his pack and a lone wolf—no place within his pack or mine. After all of this was done, he would be on his own with Rain. Abandoned. I wanted to hide him from that reality but I knew my parents would not accept him into our home after his pack had murdered our own. He would live a hindered life in the presence of the victims' relations if he stayed near.

My mind drifted to the villagers. I thought about those whom my parents had said were not faithful to our cause. No traitors had yet been revealed. I feared now I would face those wolves as they guarded the ships alongside those who had risen against us.

"Sia," Lyon's voice reached out to me, snapping me out of my thoughts. "Please look after Reina, no matter what happens to me."

I was pained by his request but I confirmed to him that I would try my very best. I wanted to protect them both, to send both of them home. But with our scent being picked up by Fimble's sister, we now walked toward what might prove our final battle.

Trim and I looked meaningfully at one another, fearful of the separation we now faced. I grabbed his hand, no longer frightened of how the others might react. He was my equal and we were walking into this fight together. I would not let anything happen to Trim. He was the one wolf I could not be without.

Chapter Twenty-Five- My Love

We assessed their numbers from the safety of some nearby trees. Some guards casually milled around but others were ready and waiting for our attack. The wind blew from the sea to land, so they would not detect our scents so easily. I searched for Taleb in the hope that maybe he was there so I could confirm his existence with my very own eyes, but much to my disappointment, he was not. There were many of them and I feared for our chances of escaping. Rain's heavy body still limped. She evaluated the numbers while reaching for her bow and arrows.

Scents quickly swept over us with the sea breeze as everyone readied themselves. I insisted that Lyon and Reina stay within the shelter of the trees. They would be close enough then for us to see if anyone attacked them. This way they were far enough away from the bloodshed but within running distance to the ships, should the opportunity present itself.

"Sia," Trim said, drawing my attention away from the wolves we were fated to fight. He cupped my face and looked at me fiercely.

He did not need to say it. I put my hand to his. "I will protect you too," I said with a small smile, holding back my tears. This battle had come far too soon. It seemed that so much had happened and we were not afforded the necessary amount of time needed to prepare ourselves. All we could do was march in with dignity to protect our land and pack. This was not something he would deny me. Although I could see he wanted to shield me from the battle, he would allow me to fight by his side as his equal. If my parents, the remainder of my pack, and those who lived in the Kingdom could have fought with us today, they would have. But with no time to summon them, I could only imagine they were with me in spirit. I felt them in my steps and accepted them as my strength. We would fight together for control of this powerful object that had the means to connect our world to that of the humans. Taleb's army had to be destroyed today before it became impossible to penetrate his guard.

"*I* will protect her," Fimble said to Trim cockily. "I will not accept defeat, Sia, so do not go dying on me prematurely." Trim's jaw clenched at the provocation. I realized now that I had seen them exchange this look many times before but I did not understand then that it was rivalry. Now I could see that they both fostered feelings for me.

"Rain, I cannot thank you enough for the years you have spent as my companion, mentoring me and challenging me. Here's to our continued path," Fimble said cheerily. Rain gave him a dismissive look, but her orange eyes glowed with appreciation of his words.

"Then shall I?" Rain quipped, pulling back three arrows on her bow. She stood alongside Trim, who took aim with two. Simultaneously they released them, triggering our attack. They hit all five of their targets. Soundlessly their victims fell to the ground. The wolves looked up in momentary surprise, but their quick reactions told us they had been waiting for this very moment.

Trim ran ahead and I followed in his footsteps. Fimble and Rain continued shooting their arrows from behind us as the wolves launched their onslaught. The small army we faced moved together as one. They were strategic and well-armed. Trim ran ahead to meet them, with me only steps behind. Within seconds I was close enough to the rival wolves to register the determination shinning in their eyes.

Trim had slashed at numerous wolves' throats before I had even reached his side. I shadowed Trim, blocking a few of them with Lady Momiko's stick and swiping at their feet to knock them to the ground. I smashed the hilt into the wolves' foreheads, swinging it around my head when I heard an arrow coming toward me.

I sensed another oncoming arrow and knocked it off its path just in time. I blocked another wolf that brought down a knife on me, then dodged to the side and kneed him in the stomach. Grabbing the knife out of his hand, I moved forward to stab it into his foot. He howled with pain as the blade sliced through his flesh.

A strangled noise rang out to my side and I saw that Trim had saved me from another wolf. Trim dug his claws deep into either side of the wolf's neck before throwing him away from me.

My eye was caught by the monstrous objects that floated near the sand. I only had a moment to take in the enormity of the ships before another wolf came forward to attack me, but an arrow pierced through his head and he fell to the sand.

Familiar honeycomb-colored hair caught my attention as Hansel stalked Trim. My heart ached to know that Hansel was one of the traitors amongst our kind. I took my pack's disappointment in him as my strength. I strode toward him, my rage building at his traitorous actions with each step I took. My father had placed trust in him to guard us with his very life. I now saw through his charismatic demeanor to his true fickle nature. I felt foolish for not having realized sooner his deceit. For how long had he planned to betray us?

Trim was making his way through the wolves that closely guarded the ships, dropping all those who stood in his path. Hansel noticed me when I swung Lady Momiko's stick at his face, deterring his attention from Trim. I missed and he countered my attack, his sword slicing the air as he focused on me. My strength was able to match his when I looked him dead in the eye. "You traitor!" I snarled. I knocked his wrist so that the sword swung away from me. I held my stick at both ends to block his sword, which he kept swiping at me. When I had an opening I aimed at his legs, but he quickly dodged to the right. I held my stick firmly at its handle as if it were a sword.

Hansel looked at me with a cunning smile. "You always did play hard to get," he sneered, stepping away from my swing. As I pulled my stick back to attack yet again he rapidly moved forward and punched me in the face. The knock startled me and there was an instant ringing in my ears. I took a step back, still swinging Lady Momiko's stick in defense.

Just as Hansel closed the distance between us, Trim skidded on the sand in front of me, deflecting Hansel's sword and then backhanding him across the face. Hansel took a few steps back, stroking his jaw as they faced one another. "You were always the one whom I truly wanted to test my strength against," Hansel smirked. They launched at one another at a rapid speed.

Footsteps nearby forced me to tear my eyes from them. A woman came for me with a long sword, which very nearly scrapped against my stomach. I jumped back and used Lady Momiko's stick again like a sword. Her strength overpowered mine and she plunged the sword through the air toward my chest. I gathered my energy to block it with my stick but the force she had put behind it caused it to glide down my face, slicing my bandage and cheek. The instant bright burst of light sent me plummeting to the ground. I could not see and I blindly swung Lady Momiko's stick around, trying to defend myself from the ground. I closed the eye and squinted through my other just in time to discover her next move. I rolled to the side, picked up a knife and threw it at her leg. I did not condone my violent action, but I could not be the weak one of our team. I would not murder, but I would protect the others.

I looked for Trim but I could not sense him anywhere nearby. I swirled frantically round to ascertain the position of my companions. A heavy migraine disorientated me but I could just make out Rain's figure. I watched in horror as four wolves mounted her. Her knee buckled under their weight and she was stabbed five times. She swiped her bow across one of their faces and pierced an arrow into another's neck.

Fimble screamed out to Rain and charged the other wolves. He slaughtered them as Rain collapsed to the ground. The sand below her was stained red. Fimble did not have the opportunity to comfort her. He rapidly shot arrows at those who swarmed him until he ran out of his supply. He used his bow as a weapon to protect Rain's unmoving body, which was now facing down in the sand.

I looked in front of me toward the ships, paralyzed by the frightful image before me. Trim fought against many wolves. They backed him toward the water. Hansel was still enthusiastically fighting him alongside another three wolves that attacked him on the side. Reina's scream echoed in my ear and I looked toward her, deranged by my fear. Two wolves had grabbed her; Lyon fought another off but he was outmatched.

They dragged Reina toward the ship. Black fur glinted in the sunlight. It was the color of my pack. I realized that Taleb had been here the whole time. Hansel gave up fighting Trim to greet him. After they exchanged a few words, Taleb looked at me for only a moment. His face was not very clear as I was blinded by my conflicting eyesight. I watched as he turned his back on me. The wolves carried Reina to his side on the ship.

Wolves crept toward me and I defended myself effectively, driven by my determination to get to Trim. Another four wolves grabbed him fiercely, pulling him back toward the water. My stick moved like an extension of my left hand. I still covered my right eye as it could not endure the daylight. I fought my hardest against the wolves to reach Trim. I injured them just enough that they could not attack me again. The wolves ahead pulled Trim onto the ship and I screamed for him to come back to me, but my vision of him blurred.

He fought and struggled against them, but he was hoisted aboard. My legs were too short to close the distance between us in time. The ship slowly pushed away from the shore as the water's current claimed it. The two ships on my right were set alight and flames licked their great wooden sides within seconds. It felt like time slowed as I reached out toward the ship that had taken Trim and Reina.

I screamed Trim's name over and over again from where I crouched in the sand. I was unable to comprehend how quickly everything had changed. No one else attacked me amidst the chaos of the ship moving off from the beach. I got to my feet and waded through the water, trying to avoid the flaming ships on either side of me. I had to get to them, had to save them. A large barrel of black liquid dropped into the water near me, followed by a lit stick. When the fire touched the black liquid, huge flames exploded in front of me and threw me backward, out of the water. I fell in and out of darkness.

*

Ringing pierced my ears. I felt like I had been coughing into the sand for days. I choked as I tried to recall who I was and why my body bled. The flames had roasted my own flesh. I began to realize the explosion had forced me onto the sand. Many dead bodies surrounded me; perhaps I was one of them. These were the others who had also been affected by such fierce flames; they were burned alive. I bordered on death—I could feel my melted skin.

"Sia," Lyon ran to me, maddened by desperation. "No, no, no... You have to get up, you have to help me get Reina," he cried.

I looked at him with both my eyes open. For the first time I could use them both simultaneously. It seemed the darkness of death itself was the remedy I needed to dim my right eye; but was it too late?

Lyon left my side. Perhaps he thought I was already dead. The sun's position had changed drastically and slowly I began to feel again. I looked up into the sky where smoke billowed. I could feel Ara licking my fingertips. Soon after that I could feel my legs, and then every inch of me that hurt. One thought magnified my pain. *Why has Taleb taken my Trim?*

My strength started to gather. I thought of Lady Momiko's words. She claimed I was given the gifts I needed, and that I had lost sight of her greatest concern. Her words echoed in my mind. She had told me to always look after Trim, but I had failed.

Slowly I was able to peel myself from the sand and pull Ara to my chest. My hearing started to focus on the things around me. The two ships on my right had burned to their foundations. The unknown liquids they contained had exploded on the water's surface, claiming the lives of those in close proximity. Why would humans equip such magnificent objects with the means to perish in the salty water?

Many of Taleb's men had been affected and only a few could move; the rest were dead. He did not care for them. He had seized control over the ship, and he had taken Reina and Trim. Perhaps he already knew how to use the ships and he was only waiting for us.

Lyon scampered back and forth on the deck of a smaller ship nearby. It had suffered some damage in the fire but somehow the flames did not do significant damage. I dragged myself to my feet, leaning heavily on Lady Momiko's stick. I once again looked over all the bodies and crinkled my nose at the smell of burned flesh. Fimble was draped lifelessly over Rain ahead of me. I limped over, hesitant to face the fact that he too might be dead. My chest tightened at the scene. He had fought for his mentor and companion, only to reach his demise alongside her.

I came to bid him farewell, but to my surprise he rose to his knees, battered and bloodied. He looked like a ghost in his grief. "She was all I had left," he whispered to himself.

I halted and lowered myself to his eyelevel. I did not want to encroach on his farewell. My voice was raw as it had not yet fully healed after the flames scorched my throat. "You have *me*," I rasped. I was not Rain and I paled in comparison to the brave wolf. But I was a companion none the less, and we were both lucky to be alive.

His knees slowly slithered through the sand as he crawled over to me. He wrapped his arms around me and lowered his head to the soft warmth of my stomach. I petted his matted gray hair for comfort. The shocking death of his closest friend caused him to wail like he were a cub once again. He was so strong and yet so sensitive. I now understood why he could not murder me when he had the chance. He valued life and his heart was pure, despite his ability to bring death upon all his opponents.

"They took Reina and Trim," I said, looking over the large body of water. I suspected they were being taken to the Forbidden Land. It was a decision we had all made to come here and weaken Taleb's defenses. Little did we realize that that was part of Taleb's plan. But why was it Reina and Trim he wanted? Why did he take only them?

"Will you try to follow them?" Fimble asked, now standing. He rested his weight on one leg. There was a severe cut on his shin and across his chest.

"I must," I replied. Lady Momiko did not have to offer guidance for me to realize what action I needed to take. She had said that I needed to figure something out on my own once before, but because I was too late it was Trim who suffered. My tears would not bring them back. I needed to follow them. He needed strength from me now. My mind raced. *I will not let them take Trim away from me. I cannot allow them to make a Phantom*

Wolf out of him. They would terrify and torture him in the world of humans that he so greatly fears. But why Trim of all wolves?

Lyon ran toward us, panting heavily. He had a bleeding ear and claw marks across his shoulder. "I can fix the ship. I need to get her back," he cried, speaking of his little sister.

"How long until it will be fixed?" I asked eagerly. I entertained the very same intention.

"Two days, tops. I need to get her back!" Lyon cried out loud again for the little sister that had been ripped away from him. All his family had been killed because of Taleb's men and now he had taken the last loved one that Lyon had. We would fight together to get them back. Firstly we would need to learn more of one another to understand our two different worlds. We would think of a way to retrieve them from the Forbidden Land—we had no other choice.

I felt distant to my usual uncertain self. I felt fierce and mighty, and I burned savagely to retrieve the wolf I loved. I no longer felt weak. I fiddled with the moonstone necklace at my chest that he had given me. I would focus purely on him. I could not cry for Trim because if I did, I would have to believe he was dead.

"We will," I said strongly. "We will follow them and get them back. Fimble?" I asked, looking at him. He looked into the distance over the sea. Would he abandon us now and live the rest of his life in loneliness?

"I no longer have anything here, and I think it was always my fate to follow you, Sia," Fimble said, looking at Rain. I mourned for her death; she would have fought to her very last breath for the protection of Fimble.

"A human, a traitor, and a royal wolf, what an eclectic pack we make," he mused.

We had some strength in our strange group, but we did not know why Taleb so patiently waited for Trim, and that destroyed my hope of having an upper hand in this fight. But as I looked through Sia's eye and my own simultaneously, I realized why I had been gifted. I needed this experience so that I could transition to a near death. I needed to complete the final phase of transitioning into a Phantom Wolf. Although I did not feel much different, my ability to use the Phantom Wolf eye suggested otherwise. My transition was now complete. To fully accept it I had to die. I would now forever be stuck with the Phantom Wolf eye, but perhaps I needed this so I could find Trim. Perhaps Lady Momiko and Sia had known this all along. They all had a purpose in Trim's life, and they indicated that I too had all the tools to help him. *She has given me this eye to aid me in finding and helping Trim, as did Lady Momiko with her premonitions. But why is Trim fated to be of such importance?*

Lady Momiko's words echoed in my mind. I could only focus on one thing, and that was to protect Trim. All the gifts I had been given were all that I needed. I felt as if my canines lengthened as my thoughts grew savage. I could taste blood in my mouth. My body had evolved to a higher strength. They had given me these gifts to specifically track and aid Trim. And as Lady Momiko had told me from a very young age, Trim was meant for greatness. All of us, including The Great Phantom Wolf, Sia, were meant to have met him. And I now knew my part in his life, whether it was here or in a new world—the human world.

Trim had taught me most of what I knew about fighting and defense. And it was now time for me to honor him by executing the skills with which he had provided me. I would not allow us to become so close only to tragically part ways.

For all my life he has protected me and chased me. Now it is time for me to return that loyalty. I have now found my own strength. And I will find Trim, because I love him. I have always loved him; I always will. A bright future is what we will walk into, but first, I must fight for him. And no obstacle will be too great for me to find him.

I will now give chase, my love. You will be my forever.

About The Author

Kia grew up in the Darling Downs Region in Queensland, Australia. Graduating High School, she pursued a career in freelance journalism. In 2014, having always had a passion for writing fiction, she decided to follow her dream of becoming an accomplished author.

Now living in Edinburgh, Scotland Kia has a can do attitude, a strong will and the touch of kindness that makes it hard not to fall in love with her. Announced 'The Best New Author of 2015' by AusRomToday, and being awarded numerous awards, she has no intentions of stopping. Kia Carrington-Russell is definitely the new author to be looking out for.

Learn more about Kia at www.kiacarrington-russell.com and follow @kia_crystal on Instagram.

Also Available

The Three Immortal Blades
Possession Of My Soul
Possession Of My Heart
Possession Of My Fate

Phantom Wolf Series
Phantom Wolf
Sia
Phantom Eye
Phantom King

Token Huntress Series
Token Huntress
Token Vampire
Token Wolf

The Shadow Minds Journal Series

My Escort Series
My Escort
My Exception
My Expectation

Taming Himself Series
Aroused
Taste

www.ingramcontent.com/pod-product-compliance
Lightning Source LLC
Chambersburg PA
CBHW030643110726
47901CB00002B/550